A Latino Boy in the United States

Paco

Margarita Robleda

Illustrated by
Danilo Ramirez P.

ALFAGUARA

Published in Spanish as *Paco, un niño latino en Estados Unidos*

© Text: 2004, Margarita Robleda

© This edition: 2004, Santillana USA Publishing Company, Inc.
2023 NW 84th Avenue
Miami, FL 33122
www.santillanausa.com

Managing Editor: Isabel Mendoza
Translation: Leland Northam
Book design by Jacqueline Rivera and Mauricio Laluz
Illustrated by Danilo Ramirez P.

Alfaguara is part of the **Santillana Group**, with offices in the following countries:
ARGENTINA, BOLIVIA, CHILE, COLOMBIA, COSTA RICA, DOMINICAN REPUBLIC,
ECUADOR, EL SALVADOR, GUATEMALA, MEXICO, PANAMA, PARAGUAY, PERU,
PUERTO RICO, SPAIN, UNITED STATES, URUGUAY, AND VENEZUELA.

ISBN 10: 1-59437-560-7
ISBN 13: 978-1-59437-560-6

Published in the United States of America
Printed in the United States of America by NuPress

15 14 13   1 2 3 4 5 6 7 8 9

For all the Williams in the world

William was four when I met him.
That was on a day that I was
invited to sing at the Benavidez
Elementary School in Houston,
Texas. I found out that he had
been at the school for six months,
and although his teacher, Mrs.
Crouch, had tried everything,
William had never opened his mouth.
After my presentation, William went

back to his classroom and said, "I can do it.
I am really smart." And he started to talk.
When I heard this, I went to meet him. William was a sweet,
sensitive boy who had been torn from his country of Guatemala,
from his language and his friends, and taken to a strange country.
Finding himself surrounded by poems, riddles, songs, and laughter
that day, William probably thought, "Wow! Now I feel at home."

Margarita Robleda

My name is Francisco, but everybody calls me Paco. I am 11 years old. My story is not very long, but I do have a lot to tell. So when the teacher asked us to write our autobiography, the laziness I feel sometimes when I have to pick up a pencil to write left me. I felt important and I decided to write a book called *The Life of Mr. Francisco Javier Ramiro Gonzalez Lopez*, which is my full name. On second thought, that is probably too long for a book title, so it might be better to call it *Paco, A Latino Boy in the United States.*

My mom says that when I was born, I looked a lot like my dad. I had his eyes and his skin color. Plus, my left big toe had the same shape as his left big toe. I looked exactly like him, without his mustache, of course.

Back then I only knew how to cry, eat, and sleep. But I did everything in a big way. I slept a lot, I ate a lot, and I cried a whole lot, too.

When I had grown a little and stopped crying, I learned how to dance, how to take a bath out of my soup bowl, how to laugh, and how to say "Ma-mommy" and "Da-daddy" and "wah-wah." At first they all thought I wanted some water, but what I was really saying was "woof-woof." That is because from the time I started to crawl, I loved to play with my dog Pinto. I think I even wanted to be like him.

I was born in San Miguel, a small city where the people speak Spanish and are cheerful and friendly. When it is somebody's birthday, we bring musicians for a serenade, and we sing a birthday song called "Las Mañanitas." If it is a kid's birthday, we have a party with a piñata, balloons, ice cream, and a special dish of rice with chicken called *arroz con pollo*.

On hot nights, people take chairs out to sit in front of their houses and tell family stories or jokes and talk about lots of things. For as long as I can remember, my grandfather has been the Story King. He leaves us all with our mouths hanging open. I like his scary stories best. My favorite is one about a weeping woman, called "La Llorona." Ugh! Just thinking about it makes my hair stand up, and I get goose bumps.

My dad decided to come to the United States because he is very smart and hard-working. What he knows how to do he does really well.

At first the change scared us a lot. My mom says that the unknown is always scary. The unknown may be scary, but having to leave the known is not easy either. I hated to leave my dog, my best friend, and everybody else behind: my godparents, my cousins, the neighbors—even the guy who sold fruit ices outside my school!

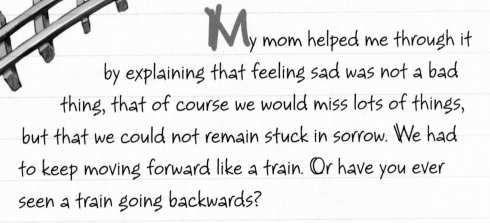

My mom helped me through it by explaining that feeling sad was not a bad thing, that of course we would miss lots of things, but that we could not remain stuck in sorrow. We had to keep moving forward like a train. Or have you ever seen a train going backwards?

My dad called a family meeting to tell us about moving to the United States. He convinced us how important it was to be positive about it, how being afraid is a waste of time, and what a great chance this was to learn a new language and a different culture.

Thinking about it now, my dad was right. He is very smart, and he says that when you stop learning it is like letting your mind retire and that has got to be really boring. That is why, while I am in school and my dad is at work, my grandpa and my mom take English and history classes. They are learning about some of the customs in this country, like Thanksgiving dinner and Halloween. The only one who has not learned anything yet is my little brother Alejandro because he is still a baby. One day I am going to tell him everything when I read him this autobiography.

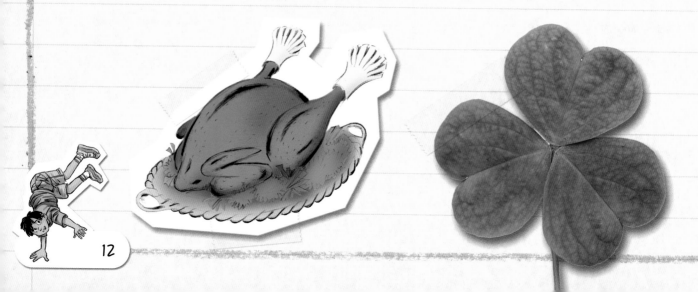

And it is true that the change was a little hard. Suddenly all the street signs were in English. That frightened us because we thought we might get lost. We could not get over how all the streets had the same name: "One Way." How funny! Why would they use the same name over and over if there were so many good names, for example, Lizard Street, Whale Avenue, General So-and-so Boulevard, or even Grandma Alicia Drive? Why use the same name for every street? Then somebody told us that "One Way" meant a street with traffic going in just one direction. Ha ha! Every time we remember that we laugh a lot.

We also thought it was strange to see stores that sold feet! Who would want to buy a foot if we have two already? Later we found out that they had lemon, apple, or pineapple flavor. And they were **pies**, which is spelled the same as the Spanish word for feet: *pies*. Ha ha!

13

In spite of the problems, little by little we got used to things. Like my grandpa says, quoting one of those old sayings he loves, "You can get used to anything except not eating." So it is no wonder that I am finding out that Italian food is delicious, almost as good as what my mom cooks. Besides, I am proud to know that corn, tomatoes, chocolate, and potatoes, among other foods that they love here, come from Latin America. We gave those delicious things to the world!

Can you imagine? Without our tomatoes, what would they use to make the ketchup that tastes so good with fries? Or what would the Italians put on their pasta and pizza? Without the chocolate we gave them, how would they make the chocolate bars we all love? Somebody here invented the hamburger, we added the potatoes, and everyone won.

Now that I am learning to read and write in English, I have found out that all languages sound different because we use different sounds. Our Spanish names have more R's, like Roberto, Rosa, and Rodrigo. Here there are more Johns, Jameses, and Janets. And there are also more words with W. One of the few that I knew before I came here was the name of my friend William.

I have already noticed that the alphabet here does not have the letter Ñ. That changes things a lot. I guess that I will have to write the words that use Ñ, like *niño*, *baño*, and *piña*, with an N: nino, bano, and pina, but they look pretty funny. In fact, they look and sound very weird. Ha ha!

My poor friend Tona wants the letter Ñ back so that she can be herself again: Toña. But the one I really feel sorry for is my neighbor Jesus Peña. In Spanish *peña* is a strong name. It means a rocky cliff. Now his last name is Pena, which is "sorrow" or "grief" in Spanish. Without the Ñ, he really does have a reason to be sad.

Anyway, I am not always making jokes. Sometimes I get homesick for the land I come from and the friends I left behind. But now I am making new friends who come from other countries where they also speak Spanish. Even though here we are called Latinos, Hispanics, Paisanos, Chicanos, Ches, or Ticos, we are like brothers and sisters because we speak the same language, and that means we stick together.

We know almost the same songs, riddles, and tongue twisters. A lot of our food is alike, and you would think that all our grandparents got together to make up the same stories. Take "La Llorona," for example. They call her by different names, but it is still the same weeping woman walking down the street in any Latin American town and yelling like a crazy person.

And when we sing the Spanish song "De Colores," we do not feel like foreigners. It is as if we are all, as the song says, "little birds that come from far away." We all belong to the same family, with the same heart.

At first, I had a hard time speaking English because I was kind of embarrassed. My hands would sweat, my stomach would go all queasy, my tongue would get thick, and my ears would turn red and feel hot.

I was sure everybody was going to laugh at me. Then I realized that they would feel the same way if they tried to speak another language.

My grandpa says, "Nothing can scare a silly donkey." I think that means that it is normal to be afraid when you have to deal with something new, and it does not make you silly. My grandpa says that we all have our own fears, too, even the people who think they are so smart. And every time somebody makes fun of somebody else it is because they are afraid that other people will make fun of them.

I do not care what anybody says or thinks now. I am proud because I know that I am learning a new language. That means I am really smart, like my dad.

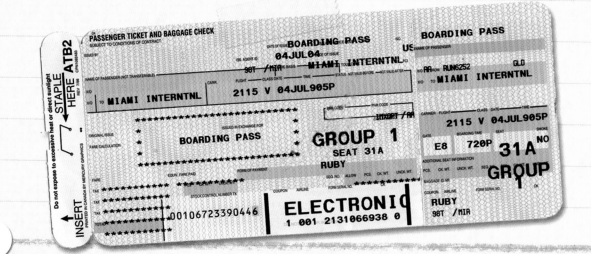

I feel a little sad sometimes when somebody calls us "wetbacks." That means that we are not from here. But my teacher Mrs. Mireles, whose family has lived here for more than five generations, told us that in this country just about everybody is an immigrant and that we come from all corners of the Earth to share the things we have inherited from our grandparents. She says that not forgetting all that makes us stronger.

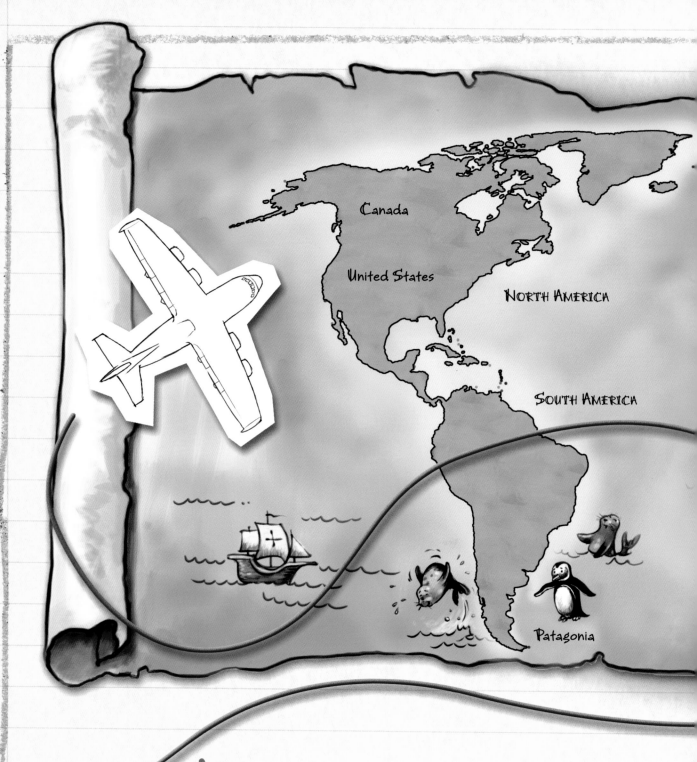

Canada

United States

NORTH AMERICA

SOUTH AMERICA

Patagonia

We come from Africa, Europe, Asia, Oceania, and from all over the Americas, from Canada to Patagonia. That is an area in Argentina and Chile near the South Pole. The word for a female duck in Spanish is *pata*, so at first I thought there were lots of ducks in Patagonia. But it does not have anything to do with ducks. Instead, Patagonia has lots of seals and penguins.

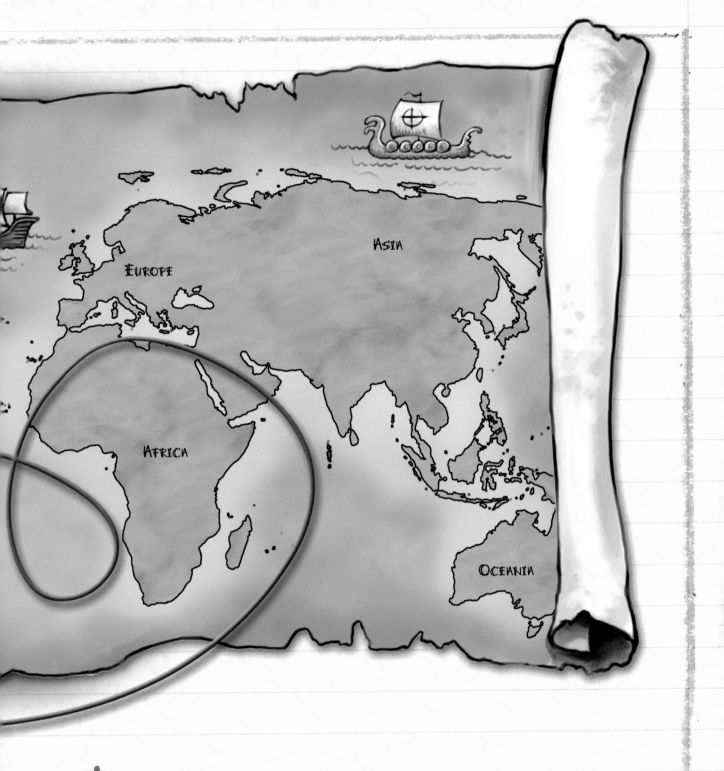

I understand now that we speak English here because the first colonists in the United States were English people. We would be speaking Spanish or French if Spaniards or French people, who got here before the English, had not given their territories to the United States later.

Or what if the Mayas had spent more time on improving their navigation? Instead, they studied the sky, invented the zero, and built fabulous temples in Guatemala, El Salvador, Honduras, Belize, and Mexico, which is what they loved to do. They could perfectly well have crossed the Gulf of Mexico and come to live where the United States of America is today. And we would see an "ek" in the night sky instead of a "star."

Back then the only people living here were Native Americans, like the Apaches and Dakotas. In social studies we learned that they lived near herds of buffalo. They followed wherever the buffalo moved to graze, so their houses were portable. How clever! Nowadays people buy so many things that moving is a little harder.

They really knew how to live at peace with the planet Earth. But we are never happy, it seems. If it gets a little hot, we turn on the air conditioning, even though in a little while we will be freezing. Then we have to put on a jacket and even light a fire in the fireplace! And then?

I wonder who was wiser, us or them?

INSTRUCTIONS

When Spain conquered Latin America, the natives were forced to speak Spanish. In those days, Mexico was much bigger. It included California, New Mexico, Arizona, Colorado, and Texas. That is why those states still have cities with Spanish names such as San Antonio, Santa Fe, Los Angeles, El Paso, Las Cruces, San Francisco, San Jose, Fresno, and on and on. It is the same in Florida, where St. Augustine is located. That is the oldest city in the United States, and the Spaniards founded it.

My grandpa likes to find Spanish names on the map. He writes them in a notebook, and when he wants to show off his English he reads them aloud. Being his grandson I am very smart, too, so I understand every word he says. Ha ha!

26

I like being Latino and bilingual and bicultural, too. I can have the best of both worlds: rice with beans plus hot dogs; tacos and empanadas plus hamburgers. Yummy! I like both American football and our *fútbol*, called "soccer" here—and baseball, too. I like celebrating the Fourth of July with all the fireworks plus the independence days of Latin American countries.

I like to sing the folk songs that my grandpa listens to, but I also like rock in Spanish and in English, and rap, too. Of all the people my teacher has made us look up, I really admire Benito Juarez and Simon Bolivar, but I also respect Abraham Lincoln a lot.

Besides, if I only spoke one language, I would not be able to understand bilingual jokes. There is one that goes, "What did one *globo* say to another *globo*?" "I globe you." Ha ha! It is really about balloons that are in love because *globo* means balloon. Well, you have to be bilingual to get it. See what I mean?

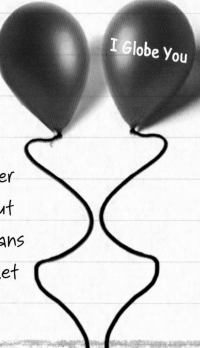

I Globe You

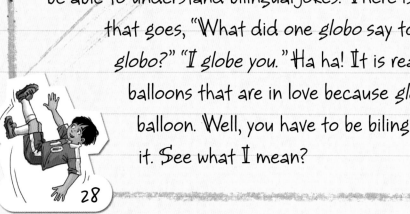

28

My grandpa says that a lot of Latin American people believe in the saying, "If you were born to be a flower pot, you will never get beyond your porch." That means that if you are born poor, you will always be poor. But he says that here that does not make much sense because this is "the land of opportunity." And what my teacher has taught us is that if you work hard, you can go very, very far.

I should definitely not have any problem going far because I am such a good runner that I might be in the Olympics one day. My mom says that if I decide to go, she will back me all the way and be there with water and oranges! I am not just fast on my feet, but I am really fast doing puzzles too. I guess that is why I am pretty quick at understanding math. In other words, I am not a flower pot at all!

What would I like to be when I grow up...besides a gentleman!? I do not know. Computers are interesting, but I like nuts and bolts too. I could be a mechanic, one of the best.

I have been thinking that if I stay in this country and do not go back to San Miguel, I might become a leader and help my community—maybe a leader who represents farm workers or other Latinos who have problems, like Cesar Chavez did in California. Maybe I could be a politician. Why not? Abraham Lincoln fought so that all men and women could be free and have the same opportunities, no matter what the color of their skin was or whether they liked to eat bread, bagels, tortillas, or arepas with their meals.

Sometimes I remember my dog Pinto and think I would like to be a veterinarian. The best thing that could happen would be to work at something I like and be useful to other people and get good pay for doing it too. What more could I wish for?

My grandpa says, "No matter how early you get up, dawn will not come any sooner." In other words, I still have a long time to think about it. What I have to do now is be positive about studying and enjoy learning new things. Every time I read a new book I imagine myself in a different job. Last night I dreamed that I was a scientist on a spaceship and that I discovered that those famous black holes in space were full of little baby black holes. Ha ha!

It is true that this is the land of opportunity, but you do not get anything for free. You have to work hard to get what you want. That is the reason we are here. We left our country, our family and neighbors, and some of our customs. But we still have our dignity, and we are proud to be good citizens. We grabbed an opportunity, and we are not going to waste it.

My grandpa says, "God takes care of those who take care of themselves." That means that things do not just fall from the sky. I am happy I come from a family of smart, hard-working people. Putting our efforts and talents together, we will get ahead.

If, as young as I am, I have lived such an interesting life, so full of adventures, I love to imagine everything that lies ahead for me to learn and enjoy. If I have done all this as just plain Paco, how about when I grow up to be Mr. Francisco Javier Ramiro Gonzalez Lopez? I will be able to write so many books like this one! I will be able to tell my grandchildren so many stories! Ha ha!

I do not know yet what I will be when I grow up. What I am sure of is that whatever I am—politician, veterinarian, mathematician, teacher, or mechanic—I want to be happy with myself, my family, and my new friends. My dad has sayings, too. He says life is not about pushing other people out of the way in order to become Number One. What I want is to be the best "me" that I can.

I finished writing this autobiography
in the dining room at home on
May 15, 2004.

Paco

amigurumi TWO!

CROCHETED TOYS FOR ME AND YOU AND BABY TOO

ana PaULa RÍMOLi

Martingale®
& COMPANY

Amigurumi Two!
Crocheted Toys for Me and You and Baby Too
© 2009 by Ana Paula Rímoli

Martingale®
& C O M P A N Y

Martingale & Company®
19021 120th Ave. NE, Suite 102
Bothell, WA 98011-9511 USA
www.martingale-pub.com

CREDITS

President & CEO ★ Tom Wierzbicki
Editor-in-Chief ★ Mary V. Green
Managing Editor ★ Tina Cook
Technical Editor ★ Ursula Reikes
Copy Editor ★ Marcy Heffernan

Design Director ★ Stan Green
Production Manager ★ Regina Girard
Illustrator ★ Laurel Strand
Cover & Text Designer ★ Regina Girard
Photographer ★ Brent Kane

Printed in China
14 13 12 11   8 7 6 5

Library of Congress Cataloging-in-Publication Data
Library of Congress Control Number: 2009003181

ISBN: 978-1-56477-922-9

MISSION STATEMENT

Dedicated to providing quality products and service to inspire creativity.

Ya sé que es tonto porque no lo vas a poder ver, pero éste es para vos papá. Te quiero mucho y te extraño siempre.

CONTENTS

iNTRODUCTiON

I have two little girls; Oli is five and Martina just turned two. What I like the most about making toys is seeing my daughters' faces when there's something I crochet that they really, really like. I watch for the surprise in their eyes when they discover a little worm inside the apple I just finished, or when they find that the turtle's belly is full of eggs waiting to hatch. I love seeing the pride in their little faces when they figure out a sorting game I just made up, or when they spend hours cuddling with their new favorite softie. In this book I tried to include toys to play with and toys to learn from. They are great little toys that would be wonderful as a present for a new baby. And you can make some of them in an evening or two and then surprise your little one in the morning with something special.

I find that after a hard (and crazy!) day, once the girls are in bed and my husband and I are just sitting around, with no energy for anything else but to watch whatever's on TV, making a nice cup of tea and choosing colors for a new toy are what relax me the most. I hope that making these little toys and decorations will be fun for you. The toys are pretty simple and straightforward to make, but most of all, they will be lots of fun for your kids to play with.

Thank you so much for buying this book and supporting my work. It means the world to me. Happy playing and happy crocheting!

—Ana

HaPPY LiTTLe aiRPLaNe

I have a love-hate relationship with airplanes. I love them because they take us home;
I hate them because it takes forever to get there. It takes over 12 hours to get from
New Jersey to Montevideo. I do like smiley, softie, toy planes, though. How cute
would it look to have a bunch of them hanging from a child's ceiling? You could
even make different sizes by making the body a little bit longer or shorter!

FiNiSHeD SiZe

Approx 8" long

MaTeRiaLS

Worsted-weight yarn in red, black,
and gray

G/6 (4 mm) crochet hook

15 mm plastic eyes with safety backings

Small pieces of white craft felt

Sewing thread and sharp needle

Black embroidery floss and tapestry
needle

Fiberfill or stuffing of your choice

PROPeLLeR

NOSE

Using black yarn,

R1: Ch 2, 5 sc in second ch from hook.

R2: Sc 2 in each sc around. (10 sts)

R3 and 4: Sc 10.

Fasten off and set aside.

BLADES

Make 2.

Using gray yarn,

R1: Ch 2, 5 sc in second ch from hook.

R2: Sc 2 in each sc around. (10 sts)

R3–9: Sc 10.

R10: Dec 5 times, sl st 1. (5 sts)

Fasten off, leaving long tail for sewing.
Sew open end tog and sew blades to
opposite sides of nose. Stuff nose a
little and set aside.

PLaNe BODY

Using red yarn,

R1: Ch 2, 5 sc in second ch from hook.

R2: Sc 2 in each sc around. (10 sts)

R3: *Sc 1, 2 sc in next sc*, rep 5 times.
(15 sts)

R4: *Sc 2, 2 sc in next sc*, rep 5 times.
(20 sts)

R5: *Sc 3, 2 sc in next sc*, rep 5 times.
(25 sts)

R6: *Sc 4, 2 sc in next sc*, rep 5 times.
(30 sts)

R7 and 8: Sc 30.

R9: *Sc 5, 2 sc in next sc*, rep 5 times.
(35 sts)

R10 and 11: Sc 35.

R12: *Sc 6, 2 sc in next sc*, rep 5 times.
(40 sts)

R13–18: Sc 40.

Sew propeller to end of plane, position
and attach eyes, embroider mouth.

R19–33: Sc 40.

R34: *Sc 6, dec 1*, rep 5 times. (35 sts)

R35: *Sc 5, dec 1*, rep 5 times. (30 sts)

R36 and 37: Sc 30.

R38: *Sc 4, dec 1*, rep 5 times. (25 sts)

R39 and 40: Sc 25.

R41: *Sc 3, dec 1*, rep 5 times. (20 sts)

Stuff almost to top.

R42: *Sc 2, dec 1*, rep 5 times. (15 sts)

R43: *Sc 1, dec 1*, rep 5 times. (10 sts)

Finish stuffing.

R44: *Sk 1 sc, sc 1*, rep 5 times. (5 sts)

Fasten off, leaving long tail to close up the 5-st hole, and weave in end.

Side Wings

Make 2.

Using red yarn,

R1: Ch 2, 8 sc in second ch from hook.

R2: Sc 2 in each sc around. (16 sts)

R3–15: Sc 16.

Fasten off, leaving long tail for sewing. Stuff lightly and sew to each side of plane.

Tail

Using red yarn,

R1: Ch 2, 7 sc in second ch from hook.

R2: Sc 2 in each sc around. (14 sts)

R3–8: Sc 14.

Fasten off, leaving long tail for sewing. Stuff lightly and sew to back of plane.

Back Wings

Make 2.

Using red yarn,

R1: Ch 2, 6 sc in second ch from hook.

R2: Sc 2 in each sc around. (12 sts)

R3–8: Sc 12.

Fasten off, leaving long tail for sewing. Stuff lightly and sew to each side at back of plane, below tail.

Finishing

Cut out little pieces of white felt for windows and sew or glue to airplane's body.

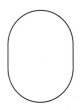

Airplane window

BRANCH MOBILE

I think the branch mobile would look pretty in front of a window, with the light shining through it. You could make it a lot more colorful also, with red birds and little purple or blue flowers. You could even turn the birds into little hanging toys for a baby's car seat or a little kid's backpack. Just put a piece of yarn through one of the stitches in the top of the head, join the two ends to form a loop, and make a little knot.

FINISHED SIZE

Approx 36" from hanging ring

MATERIALS

Worsted-weight yarn in brown, green, blue, and tiny amounts of white and yellow

F/5 (3.75 mm) and G/6 (4 mm) crochet hooks; use F hook unless stated otherwise

6 mm plastic eyes with safety backings

Small piece of tan craft felt for birds' beaks

Black embroidery floss and tapestry needle

Sewing thread and sharp needle

1 ring (mine is bamboo, approx 2½"/ 6.5 cm in diameter)

Fiberfill or stuffing of your choice

BRANCH

Using G hook and brown yarn, loosely ch 101 and join first and last sts to form a ring, being careful not to twist sts.

R1–16: Sc 100.

Fasten off, leaving long tail for sewing. Fold edges together horizontally and sew to form a donut shape, stuffing as you go.

LITTLE LEAVES

Make as many as you want.

Using G hook and green yarn, loosely ch 7, and starting at second ch from hook, sc 1, dc 1, tr 2, dc 1, sc 1; fasten off and weave in ends.

VINE AROUND BRANCH

Using G hook and green yarn, loosely ch 200; fasten off. Wrap around branch and sew in place with little leaves.

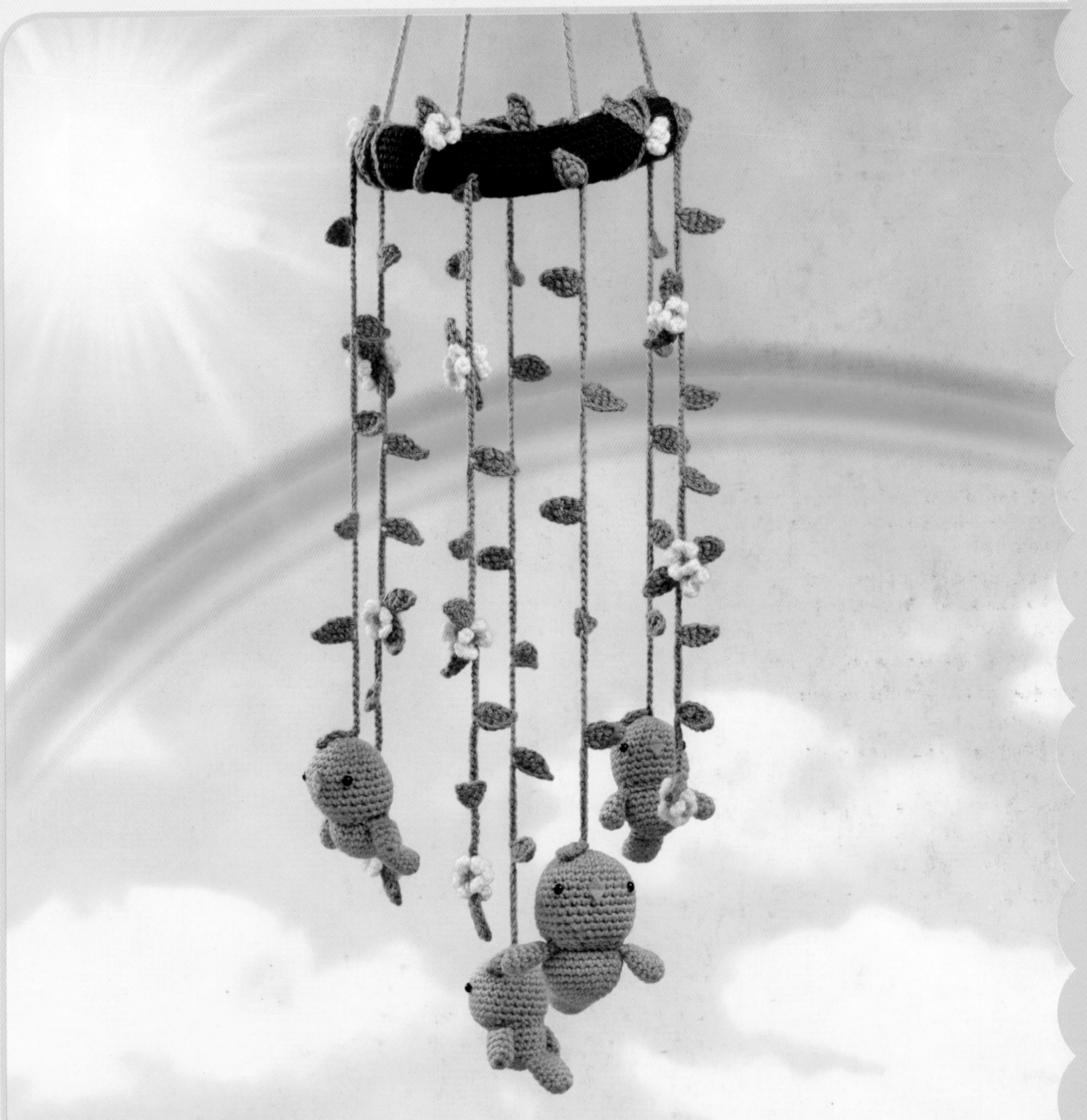

VINES FOR BIRDS

Make 4.

Using G hook and green yarn, loosely ch 7, and *starting at second ch from hook, sc 1, dc 1, tr 2, dc 1, sc 1, loosely ch 17*, rep from * to * 5 times, and starting at second ch from hook, sc 1, dc 1, tr 2, dc 1, sc 1. There will be 7 leaves on each vine. Fasten off and sew one end of leaf to branch.

VINES FOR FLOWERS

Make 4.

Using G hook and green yarn, [*loosely ch 7, and starting at second ch from hook, sc 1, dc 1, tr 2, dc 1, sc 1*, rep from * to * 1 more time, **loosely ch 17, and starting at second ch from hook, sc 1, dc 1, tr 2, dc 1, sc 1**, rep from ** to ** 1 time, loosely chain 10], rep instructions between brackets [ ] 1 more time; rep from * to * 2 times, ***loosely ch 17, and starting at second ch from hook, sc 1, dc 1, tr 2, dc 1, sc 1, rep from *** 1 more time.

FLOWERS

Make as many as you want and sew to vines and branch.

Using G hook and white yarn, *ch 4, hdc 1 in third ch from hook, sl st 1*, rep 5 times (5 petals). Sew petals together to form flower. Using yellow yarn and sewing in center of flowers, sew

2 flowers at double set of leaves on vine, and single flowers on branch.

BIG BIRD

Make 1.

Use blue yarn for bird.

HEAD

R1: Ch 2, 5 sc in second ch from hook.

R2: Sc 2 in each sc around. (10 sts)

R3: *Sc 1, 2 sc in next sc*, rep 5 times. (15 sts)

R4: *Sc 2, 2 sc in next sc*, rep 5 times. (20 sts)

R5: *Sc 3, 2 sc in next sc*, rep 5 times. (25 sts)

R6: *Sc 4, 2 sc in next sc*, rep 5 times. (30 sts)

R7–14: Sc 30.

R15: *Sc 4, dec 1*, rep 5 times. (25 sts)

R16: *Sc 3, dec 1*, rep 5 times. (20 sts)

Work on face: Position and attach eyes, cut a diamond shape from felt, fold in half, and sew to face.

R17: *Sc 2, dec 1*, rep 5 times. (15 sts)

R18: *Sc 1, dec 1*, rep 5 times. (10 sts)

Stuff head firmly.

R19: *Sk 1 sc, sc 1*, rep 5 times. (5 sts)

Fasten off, weave in end.

BODY

R1: Ch 2, 5 sc in second ch from hook.

R2: Sc 2 in each sc around. (10 sts)

R3: *Sc 1, 2 sc in next sc*, rep 5 times. (15 sts)

R4: *Sc 2, 2 sc in next sc*, rep 5 times. (20 sts)

R5: *Sc 3, 2 sc in next sc*, rep 5 times. (25 sts)

R6–10: Sc 25.

Fasten off, leaving long tail for sewing. Stuff and sew to head.

TAIL

R1: Sc 2, 6 sc in second ch from hook.

R2: Sc 2 in each sc around. (12 sts)

R3–9: Sc 12.

Fasten off, leaving long tail for sewing. Sew open end tog and sew to body.

WINGS

Make 2.

R1: Ch 2, 5 sc in second ch from hook.

R2: Sc 2 in each sc around. (10 sts)

R3–7: Sc 10.

Fasten off, leaving long tail for sewing. Sew open end tog and sew to body.

LITTLE BIRDS

Make 3.

Use blue yarn for all birds.

HEAD

R1: Ch 2, sc 5 in second ch from hook.

R2: Sc 2 in each sc around. (10 sts)

R3: *Sc 1, 2 sc in next sc*, rep 5 times. (15 sts)

R4: *Sc 2, 2 sc in next sc*, rep 5 times. (20 sts)

R5: *Sc 3, 2 sc in next sc*, rep 5 times. (25 sts)

R6–12: Sc 25.

R13: *Sc 3, dec 1*, rep 5 times. (20 sts)

Work on face: Position and attach eyes, cut a diamond shape from felt, fold in half, and sew to face.

R14: *Sc 2, dec 1*, rep 5 times. (15 sts)

R15: *Sc 1, dec 1*, rep 5 times. (10 sts)
Stuff head firmly.

R16: *Sk 1 sc, sc 1*, rep 5 times. (5 sts)
Fasten off and weave in end.

BODY

R1: Ch 2, sc 5 in second ch from hook.

R2: Sc 2 in each sc around. (10 sts)

R3: *Sc 1, 2 sc in next sc*, rep 5 times. (15 sts)

R4: *Sc 2, 2 sc in next sc*, rep 5 times. (20 sts)

R5–8: Sc 20.

Fasten off, leaving long tail for sewing. Stuff and sew to head.

TAIL

R1: Ch 2, sc 5 in second ch from hook.

R2: Sc 2 in each sc around. (10 sts)

R3–7: Sc 10.

Fasten off, leaving long tail for sewing. Sew open end tog and sew to body.

WINGS

Make 2 for each bird.

R1: Ch 2, sc 8 in second ch from hook.

R2–5: Sc 8.

Fasten off, leaving long tail for sewing. Sew open end tog and sew to body.

FINISHING

Sew bottom leaf of vines to top of each bird's head.

To cover ring: Tie yellow yarn around ring, knot, insert G hook through ring, YO, bring hook toward you, and sc 1 to form loop around ring. Rep as many times as needed to cover ring.

To hang ring from branch: Loosely ch 60, fasten off leaving long tail for sewing. Make 4 chains. Sew all four chains to ring. Sew other ends equal distance apart to branch.

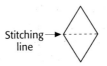

Stitching line

Bird beak

HOT-AiR BaLLOON

When I was a little girl, I always thought it would be the best to fly in a hot-air balloon and see the beach and my house from up there. This little bear is a lot luckier, though, because he gets to see Oli and Martina when they're playing in their room.

FiNiSHED SiZE

Approx 12" from top of balloon to bottom of basket

MaTERiaLS

Worsted-weight yarn in purple, yellow, orange, red, green, brown, and white

F/5 (3.75 mm) and G/6 (4 mm) crochet hooks

6 mm plastic eyes with safety backings

Black embroidery floss and tapestry needle

Fiberfill or stuffing of your choice

BaLLOON

Using G and purple yarn,

R1: Ch 2, 5 sc in second ch from hook.

R2: Sc 2 in each sc around. (10 sts)

R3: *Sc 1, 2 sc in next sc*, rep 5 times. (15 sts)

Change to yellow yarn.

R4: *Sc 2, 2 sc in next sc*, rep 5 times. (20 sts)

R5: *Sc 3, 2 sc in next sc*, rep 5 times. (25 sts)

R6: *Sc 4, 2 sc in next sc*, rep 5 times. (30 sts)

Change to orange yarn.

R7: *Sc 5, 2 sc in next sc*, rep 5 times. (35 sts)

R8: *Sc 6, 2 sc in next sc*, rep 5 times. (40 sts)

R9: *Sc 7, 2 sc in next sc*, rep 5 times. (45 sts)

Change to red yarn.

R10: *Sc 8, 2 sc in next sc*, rep 5 times. (50 sts)

R11: *Sc 9, 2 sc in next sc*, rep 5 times. (55 sts)

R12: *Sc 10, 2 sc in next sc*, rep 5 times. (60 sts)

Change to green yarn.

R13–15: Sc 60.

Change to purple yarn.

R16–18: Sc 60.

Change to yellow yarn.

R19–21: Sc 60.

Change to orange yarn.

R22: *Sc 10, dec 1*, rep 5 times. (55 sts)

R23: Sc 55.

R24: *Sc 9, dec 1*, rep 5 times. (50 sts)

Change to red yarn.

R25: Sc 50.

R26: *Sc 8, dec 1*, rep 5 times. (45 sts)

R27: Sc 45.

Change to green yarn.

R28: *Sc 7, dec 1*, rep 5 times. (40 sts)

R29: Sc 40.

R30: *Sc 6, dec 1*, rep 5 times. (35 sts)

Change to purple yarn.

R31: Sc 35.

R32: *Sc 5, dec 1*, rep 5 times. (30 sts)

R33: Sc 30.

Change to yellow yarn.

R34: *Sc 4, dec 1*, rep 5 times. (25 sts)

R35 and 36: Sc 25.

Fasten off and weave in end.

BOTTOM CIRCLE

(to close bottom of balloon)

Using orange yarn,

R1: Ch 2, 5 sc in second ch from hook.

R2: Sc 2 in each sc around. (10 sts)

R3: *Sc 1, 2 sc in next sc*, rep 5 times. (15 sts)

R4: *Sc 2, 2 sc in next sc*, rep 5 times. (20 sts)

R5: *Sc 3, 2 sc in next sc*, rep 5 times. (25 sts)

Fasten off, leaving long tail for sewing. Stuff balloon almost to top and line up sts of circle with sts of open end of balloon, sew three-quarters of the way around, finish stuffing, and finish sewing. Weave in end.

Basket

Using G hook and brown yarn,

R1: Ch 2, 7 sc in second ch from hook.

R2: Sc 2 in each sc around. (14 sts)

R3: *Sc 1, 2 sc in next sc*, rep 7 times. (21 sts)

R4: *Sc 2, 2 sc in next sc*, rep 7 times. (28 sts)

R5: *Sc 3, 2 sc in next sc*, rep 7 times. (35 sts)

R6–12: Sc 35.

Fasten off and weave in end.

Bear

Use F hook and white yarn for bear.

MUZZLE

R1: Ch 2, 5 sc in second ch from hook.

R2: Sc 2 in each sc around. (10 sts)

R3: *Sc 1, 2 sc in next sc*, rep 5 times. (15 sts)

R4: Sc 15.

Fasten off, leaving long tail for sewing. Embroider nose and mouth and set aside.

HEAD

R1: Ch 2, 6 sc in second ch from hook.

R2: Sc 2 in each sc around. (12 sts)

R3: *Sc 1, 2 sc in next sc*, rep 6 times. (18 sts)

R4: *Sc 2, 2 sc in next sc*, rep 6 times. (24 sts)

R5: *Sc 3, 2 sc in next sc*, rep 6 times. (30 sts)

R6–13: Sc 30.

R14: *Sc 3, dec 1*, rep 6 times. (24 sts)

R15: *Sc 2, dec 1*, rep 6 times. (18 sts)

Work on face: Position and attach eyes, sew muzzle in place. Stuff head almost to top.

R16: *Sc 1, dec 1*, rep 6 times. (12 sts)

R17: Dec 6 times. (6 sts)

Fasten off and weave in end.

EARS

Make 2.

R1: Ch 3, 6 hdc in third ch from hook.

Fasten off, leaving long tail for sewing. Sew to head and weave in end.

BODY

R1: Ch 2, 6 sc in second ch from hook.

R2: Sc 2 in each sc around. (12 sts)

R3: *Sc 1, 2 sc in next sc*, rep 6 times. (18 sts)

R4–7: Sc 18.

Fasten off, leaving long tail for sewing. Stuff and sew to head.

ARMS AND LEGS

Make 2 of each.

R1: Ch 2, 6 sc in second ch from hook.

R2–6: Sc 6.

Fasten off, leaving long tail for sewing. Sew open end tog, sew to body, and weave in end.

Finishing

Cut 3 pieces of yarn (I used purple), each about 8" long. Sew pieces of yarn equidistant from each other around top of basket. Tie other ends of each yarn piece to bottom circle of balloon, also equidistant from each other.

To hang balloon, cut a piece of yarn twice as long as you want the little balloon to hang. Fold yarn in half, insert folded end into sts at top of balloon, and pull ends through. Knot ends and hang it wherever you want!

Tuck little bear into basket.

STROLLER TOYS

When Oli and Martina were little, we got them a couple of stroller toys, and they never really played with them (whatever they were looking at outside was a lot more interesting and fun). They were, however, into whatever random toy I would hang from the stroller with a long piece of yarn—go figure.

These stroller toys would make a cute and original handmade present for a new baby. They're both colorful and fun to look at, and they are a great way to encourage talking about different colors and counting! They could also be hooked to a crib or car seat.

FINISHED SIZE

Approx 10" long from hanging loop to bottom of flower or fish

MATERIALS

Worsted-weight yarn in green, yellow, white, orange, red, and blue

F/5 (3.75 mm) crochet hook

6 mm (for flowers) and 9 mm (for fish) plastic eyes with safety backings

Black embroidery floss and tapestry needle

Fiberfill or stuffing of your choice

Two little pieces of Velcro with sticky back for each toy

STROLLER RING

Use green yarn for garden toy and blue yarn for fish toy.

Loosely ch 45.

R1: Sc 44, starting in second ch from hook.

R2 and 3: Ch 1, sc 44.

Fasten off and weave in end. Put a piece of Velcro on each end so that they face each other to close.

STEMS TO HOLD FLOWERS AND FISH

Use green yarn for garden toy and blue yarn for fish toy.

LONG STEM

Make 1.

Loosely ch 51, sl st 50, starting at second ch from hook. Fasten off, leaving long tail for sewing.

SHORT STEM

Make 2.

Loosely ch 41, sl st 40, starting at second ch from hook. Fasten off, leaving long tail for sewing.

Sew one end of stem around stroller ring so that stem can move.

You'll sew fish or flowers to other end.

GARDEN FLOWERS

CENTER

Make 3.

Using yellow yarn,

R1: Ch 2, 5 sc in second ch from hook.

R2: Sc 2 in each sc around. (10 sts)

R3: *Sc 1, 2 sc in next sc*, rep 5 times. (15 sts)

R4: *Sc 2, 2 sc in next sc*, rep 5 times. (20 sts)

R5: *Sc 3, 2 sc in next sc*, rep 5 times. (25 sts)

Work on face: Position and attach eyes, embroider mouth.

R6: *Sc 4, 2 sc in next sc*, rep 5 times. (30 sts)

R7–12: Sc 30.

R13: *Sc 4, dec 1*, rep 5 times. (25 sts)

R14: *Sc 3, dec 1*, rep 5 times. (20 sts)

R15: *Sc 2, dec 1*, rep 5 times. (15 sts)

R16: *Sc 1, dec 1*, rep 5 times. (10 sts)

R17: *Sk 1 sc, sc 1*, rep 5 times. (5 sts)

Fasten off and weave in end.

PETALS

Make 7 for each flower.

Using red or white yarn,

R1: Ch 2, 6 sc in second ch from hook.

R2: Sc 2 in each sc around. (12 sts)

R3–6: Sc 12.

Fasten off, leaving long tail for sewing. Sew open end tog and sew 7 petals to flower center. Sew 1 flower to end of each green stem.

LEAF

Make 3.

Using green yarn,

R1: Ch 2, 5 sc in second ch from hook.

R2: Sc 2 in each sc around. (10 sts)

R3: Sc 10.

R4: *Sc 1, 2 sc in next sc*, rep 5 times. (15 sts)

R5: Sc 15.

R6: *Sc 2, 2 sc in next sc*, rep 5 times. (20 sts)

R7: *Sc 2, dec 1*, rep 5 times. (15 sts)

R8: Sc 15.

R9: *Sc 1, dec 1*, rep 5 times. (10 sts)

R10: Sc 10.

R11: *Sk 1 sc, sc 1*, rep 5 times. (5 sts)

Fasten off, leaving long tail for sewing. Sew open end tog and sew 1 leaf to each green stem as desired.

FISH IN THE SEA

BODY

Make 3.

Using desired yarn color,

R1: Ch 2, 5 sc in second ch from hook.

R2: Sc 2 in each sc around. (10 sts)

R3: *Sc 1, 2 sc in next sc*, rep 5 times. (15 sts)

R4: Sc 15.

R5: *Sc 2, 2 sc in next sc*, rep 5 times. (20 sts)

R6: Sc 20.

R7: *Sc 3, 2 sc in next sc*, rep 5 times. (25 sts)

R8–12: Sc 25.

Work on face: Position and attach eyes, embroider mouth.

R13–16: Sc 25.

R17: *Sc 3, dec 1*, rep 5 times. (20 sts)

R18: *Sc 2, dec 1*, rep 5 times. (15 sts)

Stuff almost to top.

R19: *Sc 1, dec 1*, rep 5 times. (10 sts)

Finish stuffing.

R20: *Sk 1 sc, sc 1*, rep 5 times. (5 sts)

Fasten off and weave in end.

TAIL

Make 2 pieces for each tail; make 3 tails.

Using colors to match fish bodies,

R1: Ch 2, 5 sc in second ch from hook.

R2: Sc 2 in each sc around. (10 sts)

R3–7: Sc 10.

R8: Dec 5 times. (5 sts)

R9: Sc 5.

Fasten off, leaving long tail for sewing. Sew 2 pieces of tail next to each other at end of body. Sew one fish to end of each blue stem.

ALGAE

Make 3.

Loosely ch 52, and starting at third ch from hook, dc 50, then loosely ch 57, and starting in second ch from hook, sc 56.

Fasten off, leaving long tail for sewing. Fold where dc and sc meet and sew this midpoint to blue chain that is attached to stroller ring.

FINISHING

Attach ring to stroller.

RaTTLeS

Every baby needs a rattle, and my girls' favorite ones were always the donut-shaped ones, probably because they were the easiest to hold. Why not make the baby in your life a couple of super-cute ones?

FINISHED SIZE

Approx 3" diameter ring

MATERIALS

Worsted-weight yarn in brown, orange, yellow, blue, white, red, green, gray, and black

F/5 (3.75 mm) crochet hook

6 mm plastic eyes with safety backings

Small pieces of tan and white craft felt (for panda bear, bunny, and cat)

Sewing thread and sharp needle

Black, brown, and pink embroidery floss and tapestry needle

Fiberfill or stuffing of your choice

Jingle bells or rattles

MAIN PART

(Donut Shape)

Using desired yarn color,

Loosely ch 45.

R1: Join first and last sts with sl st to form a ring, being careful not to twist sts, and sc 45.

R2–11: Sc 45.

Fasten off, leaving long tail for sewing. Fold piece and sew edges together to form a donut shape, stuffing as you go.

HEAD

(Rattle Part)

Using brown, white, gray, or yellow yarn,

R1: Ch 2, 5 sc in second ch from hook.

R2: Sc 2 in each sc around. (10 sts)

R3: *Sc 1, 2 sc in next sc*, rep 5 times. (15 sts)

R4: *Sc 2, 2 sc in next sc*, rep 5 times. (20 sts)

R5: *Sc 3, 2 sc in next sc*, rep 5 times. (25 sts)

R6–11: Sc 25.

Work on face: Position and attach eyes. Depending on the animal you're making, sew felt piece or beak and wings. Insert jingle bell or rattle.

R12: *Sc 3, dec 1*, rep 5 times. (20 sts)

R13: *Sc 2, dec 1*, rep 5 times. (15 sts)

R14: *Sc 1, dec 1*, rep 5 times. (10 sts)

Stuff firmly.

R15: *Sk 1 sc, sc 1*, rep 5 times. (5 sts)

Fasten off, leaving long tail for sewing. Sew to donut shape.

PANDA BEAR AND BUNNY EARS

Make 2.

Using black or gray yarn,

R1: Ch 2, 6 sc in second ch from hook.

For panda bear:

R2: Sc 6.

Fasten off, leaving long tail for sewing. Sew open end tog and sew to head.

For bunny:

R2–4: Sc 6.

Fasten off, leaving long tail for sewing. Sew open end tog and sew to head.

CAT EARS

Make 2.

Using brown yarn,

R1: Ch 2, 4 sc in second ch from hook.

R2: Sc 4.

R3: Sc 2 in each sc around. (8 sts)

Fasten off, leaving long tail for sewing. Sew open end tog and sew to head.

DUCK BEAK

Using orange yarn,

R1: Ch 2, sc 8 in second ch from hook.

R2: Sc 8.

Fasten off, leaving long tail for sewing. Sew to head.

DUCK WINGS

Make 2.

Using yellow yarn,

R1: Ch 2, sc 6 in second ch from hook.

R2 and 3: Sc 6.

Fasten off, leaving long tail for sewing. Sew open end tog and sew to body.

CREATIVE OPTION

You could also use the rattle head on wrist rattles. Just crochet a skinny rectangular piece, sew the rattle head to it, and join the ends with Velcro.

Panda bear muzzle

Bunny muzzle

Cat muzzle

TOYS IN PAJAMAS (BUNNY, BEAR, KOALA)

I love kids in footed pajamas! The cutest pictures of the girls are of them with their footed pajamas on, looking all sleepy and cuddly. What's cuter than little kids in pajamas? Softies in pajamas, of course, with their very own little good-night toys.

FINISHED SIZES

Big Toys: Approx 9" tall
Little Toys: Approx 4" tall

MATERIALS

Worsted-weight yarn in red, white, gray, pink, brown, and yellow

G/6 (4 mm) crochet hook

6, 9, or 12 mm plastic eyes with safety backings

Small pieces of black, white, pink, and tan craft felt

Sewing thread and sharp needle

Black and pink embroidery floss and tapestry needle

Small buttons for pajamas (optional)

Fiberfill or stuffing of your choice

BIG TOYS

HEAD

Using white, brown, or gray yarn,

R1: Ch 2, 6 sc in second ch from hook.

R2: Sc 2 in each sc around. (12 sts)

R3: *Sc 1, 2 sc in next sc*, rep 6 times. (18 sts)

R4: *Sc 2, 2 sc in next sc*, rep 6 times. (24 sts)

R5: *Sc 3, 2 sc in next sc*, rep 6 times. (30 sts)

R6: *Sc 4, 2 sc in next sc*, rep 6 times. (36 sts)

R7: *Sc 5, 2 sc in next sc*, rep 6 times. (42 sts)

R8: *Sc 6, 2 sc in next sc*, rep 6 times. (48 sts)

R9–20: Sc 48.

R21: *Sc 6, dec 1*, rep 6 times. (42 sts)

R22: *Sc 5, dec 1*, rep 6 times. (36 sts)

R23: *Sc 4, dec 1*, rep 6 times. (30 sts)

R24: *Sc 3, dec 1*, rep 6 times. (24 sts)

R25: Sc 24.

Work on face: For all, position and attach 9 mm eyes. For bunny or bear, cut a piece of white or tan felt, embroider nose and mouth, and sew to face. For koala, cut a piece of black felt for nose, sew to face, and embroider mouth.

R26: *Sc 2, dec 1*, rep 6 times. (18 sts)

R27: Sc 18.

Stuff head firmly.

R28: *Sc 1, dec 1*, rep 6 times. (12 sts)

R29: *Sk 1 sc, sc 1*, rep 6 times. (6 sts)

Fasten off and weave in end.

BODY

Use preferred yarn color for pajamas. If desired, work rnds 13–16 in white for stripe on koala pajamas.

R1: Ch 2, 6 sc in second ch from hook.

R2: Sc 2 in each sc around. (12 sts)

R3: *Sc 1, 2 sc in next sc*, rep 6 times. (18 sts)

R4: *Sc 2, 2 sc in next sc*, rep 6 times. (24 sts)

R5: *Sc 3, 2 sc in next sc*, rep 6 times. (30 sts)

R6: *Sc 4, 2 sc in next sc*, rep 6 times. (36 sts)

R7–14: Sc 36.

R15: *Sc 4, dec 1*, rep 6 times. (30 sts)

R16–21: Sc 30.

Fasten off, leaving long tail for sewing. Stuff and sew to head. Sew two little buttons to pajamas if you wish—they look cute.

HOOD FOR BEAR

Using yarn color to match pajamas,

R1: Ch 2, 6 sc in second ch from hook.

R2: Sc 2 in each st around. (12 sts)

R3: *Sc 1, 2 sc in next sc*, rep 6 times. (18 sts)

R4: *Sc 2, 2 sc in next sc*, rep 6 times. (24 sts)

R5: *Sc 3, 2 sc in next sc*, rep 6 times. (30 sts)

R6: *Sc 4, 2 sc in next sc*, rep 6 times. (36 sts)

R7: *Sc 5, 2 sc in next sc*, rep 6 times. (42 sts)

R8: *Sc 6, 2 sc in next sc*, rep 6 times. (48 sts)

R9–20: Sc 48.

Fasten off, leaving long tail for sewing. Position hood on bear's head, making sure the back touches the body (see photo below), sew to head and back of body (so it looks like it's a real hood).

BEAR EARS

Make 2.

Using brown yarn,

R1: Ch 2, 6 sc in second ch from hook.

R2: Sc 2 in each sc around. (12 sts)

R3: *Sc 1, 2 sc in next sc*, rep 6 times. (18 sts)

R4–7: Sc 18.

Fasten off, leaving long tail for sewing. Sew open end tog and sew on top of hood.

BUNNY EARS

Make 2.

Using white yarn,

Loosely ch 30.

R1: Hdc 28 starting in third bump at back of chain (see page 77), and then work 28 hdc on opposite side of chain (front loops of chain). (56 sts)

R2: *Hdc 4 in first sc, hdc 27*, rep once.

Fasten off, leaving long tail for sewing. Sew white felt lining to ear and sew to head.

KOALA EARS

Make 2.

Using gray yarn,

R1: Ch 2, 6 sc in second ch from hook.

R2: Sc 2 in each sc around. (12 sts)

R3: *Sc 1, 2 sc in next sc*, rep 6 times. (18 sts)

R4: *Sc 2, 2 sc in next sc*, rep 6 times. (24 sts)

R5–8: Sc 24.

Fasten off, leaving long tail for sewing. Sew open end tog and sew to head.

ARMS

Make 2.

Using white, brown, or gray yarn,

R1: Ch 2, 6 sc in second ch from hook.

R2: Sc 2 in each sc around. (12 sts)

R3: *Sc 1, 2 sc in next sc*, rep 6 times. (18 sts)

R4–6: Sc 18.

R7: *Sc 1, dec 1*, rep 6 times. (12 sts)

Change to pajama color,

R8: Sc 12.

R9: BPsc 12.

R10–21: Sc 12.

Fasten off, leaving long tail for sewing. Stuff, sew open end tog, and sew to body.

LEGS

Make 2.

Using yarn color to match pajamas,

R1: Ch 2, 6 sc in second ch from hook.

R2: Sc 2 in each sc around. (12 sts)

R3: *Sc 1, 2 sc in next sc*, rep 6 times. (18 sts)

R4: *Sc 2, 2 sc in next sc*, rep 6 times. (24 sts)

R5: Sc 24.

R6: Dc 6, sc 18.

R7: Hdc 6, sc 18.

R8: *Sc 2, dec 1*, rep 6 times. (18 sts)

R9: *Sc 1, dec 1*, rep 6 times. (12 sts)

R10–18: Sc 12.

Fasten off, leaving long tail for sewing. Stuff and sew to body.

LiTTLE ToYS

HEAD

Using white, brown, or gray yarn,

R1: Ch 2, 6 sc in second ch from hook.

R2: Sc 2 in each sc around. (12 sts)

R3: *Sc 1, 2 sc in next sc*, rep 6 times. (18 sts)

R4: *Sc 2, 2 sc in next sc*, rep 6 times. (24 sts)

R5: *Sc 3, 2 sc in next sc*, rep 6 times. (30 sts)

R6–13: Sc 30.

R14: *Sc 3, dec 1*, rep 6 times. (24 sts)

Work on face: Position and attach 6, 9, or 12 mm eyes. For bunny or bear, cut a piece of white or tan felt, embroider nose and mouth, and sew to face. For koala, cut a piece of black felt for nose, sew to face, and embroider mouth.

R15: *Sc 2, dec 1*, rep 6 times. (18 sts)

R16: *Sc 1, dec 1*, rep 6 times. (12 sts) Stuff firmly.

R17: *Sk 1 st, sc 1*, rep 6 times. (6 sts) Fasten off and weave in end.

BODY

Using white, brown, or gray yarn,

R1: Ch 2, 6 sc in second ch from hook.

R2: Sc 2 in each sc around. (12 sts)

R3: *Sc 1, 2 sc in next sc*, rep 6 times. (18 sts)

R4–7: Sc 18.

Fasten off, leaving long tail for sewing. Stuff and sew to head.

ARMS AND LEGS

Make 2 of each.

Using white, brown, or gray yarn,

R1: Ch 2, 6 sc in second ch from hook.

R2–5: Sc 6.

Fasten off, leaving long tail for sewing. Sew open end tog and sew to body.

BUNNY EARS

Make 2.

Using white yarn,

Loosely ch 15.

R1: Hdc 12 starting in third bump at back of chain (see page 77), and then work 12 hdc on opposite side of chain (front loops of chain). (24 sts)

Fasten off, leaving long tail for sewing. Cut and sew pink felt lining to ears and sew to head.

KOALA EARS

Make 2.

Using gray yarn,

R1: Ch 2, 5 sc in second ch from hook.

R2: Sc 2 in each sc around. (10 sts)

R3: *Sc 1, sc 2 in next sc*, rep 5 times. (15 sts)

R4–6: Sc 15.

Fasten off, leaving long tail for sewing. Sew open end tog and sew to head.

BEAR EARS

Make 2.

Using brown yarn,

R1: Ch 2, 6 sc in second ch from hook.

R2: Sc 2 in each sc around. (12 sts)

R3 and 4: Sc 12.

Fasten off, leaving long tail for sewing.
Sew open end tog and sew to head.

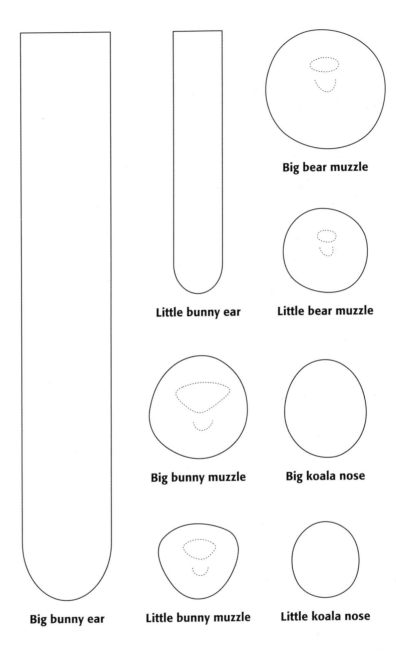

Big bear muzzle

Little bunny ear

Little bear muzzle

Big bunny muzzle

Big koala nose

Little bunny muzzle

Little koala nose

Big bunny ear

TOOL SET

I'm a girl and an only child, and I have two girls, so thinking of toys for boys doesn't always come easy for me. My husband suggested the tool set, and I loved the idea! It was so cute when I gave them to Martina for "quality control" and she started kissing the hammer, asked "him" if he was sleepy, and put him to bed! I ended up making her a set without the eyes, and she's been fixing everything around here! So decide if you want the eyes or not and make a tool set for your favorite girl or boy.

FINISHED SIZES

Screwdriver: Approx 6½" long

File: Approx 7" long

Pliers: Approx 6" long

Hammer: Approx 7½" long

MATERIALS

Worsted-weight yarn in orange, green, and gray

F/5 (3.75) crochet hook

6 mm and 9 mm plastic eyes with safety backings

Black embroidery floss and tapestry needle

Fiberfill or stuffing of your choice

SCREWDRIVER AND FILE

HANDLE

Make 1 for each tool.

Using orange yarn,

R1: Ch 2, 7 sc in second ch from hook.

R2: Sc 2 in each sc around. (14 sts)

R3–7: Sc 14.

SCREWDRIVER

Using gray yarn,

Loosely ch 7.

R1: Sc 6 starting in second bump at back of chain (see page 77), and then work 6 sc on opposite side of chain (front loops of chain). (12 sts)

Work on face: Position and attach 6 mm eyes; embroider mouth.

R8–20: Sc 14, stuffing as you go.

R21: Sc 14 through back loops only.

R22: Dec 7 times. (7 sts)

Sl st 1, fasten off, leaving long tail to close up the 7-st hole, weave in end.

R2–4: Sc 12.

R5: *Sc 1, dec 1*, rep 4 times. (8 sts)

R6–18: Sc 8, stuffing as you go.

Sl st 1, fasten off, leaving long tail for sewing. Sew to handle.

FILE

Using gray yarn,

Loosely ch 7.

R1: Sc 6 starting in second bump at back of chain (see page 77), and then work 6 sc on opposite side of chain (front loops of chain). (12 sts)

R2–20: Sc 12.

R21: *Sc 1, dec 1*, rep 4 times. (8 sts)

R22: Sc 8.

Fasten off, leaving long tail for sewing. Sew to handle.

R44: Sc 16 through back loops only.

R45: Dec 8 times. (8 sts)

Sl st 1, fasten off, leaving long tail to close up the little 8-st hole, weave in end.

HEAD

Using gray yarn,

R1: Ch 2, 8 sc in second chain from hook.

R2: Sc 2 in each sc around. (16 sts)

R3: *Sc 1, 2 sc in next sc*, rep 8 times. (24 sts)

R4: Through back loops only, *sc 1, dec 1*, rep 8 times. (16 sts)

R5–7: Sc 16.

R8: Sc 16 through back loops only.

Stuff.

R9: Dec 8 times. (8 sts)

R10: Sc 8 through front loops only.

R11: Sc 8.

Sl st 1, fasten off, leaving long tail for sewing. Finish stuffing and sew to gray portion of hammer.

NAIL TAKER-OUTER

Claw—make 2.

Using gray yarn,

R1: Ch 2, 3 sc in second ch from hook.

R2: Sc 3.

R3: Sc 2 in each sc around. (6 sts)

R4–7: Sc 6.

Sl st 1, fasten off, leaving long tail for sewing. Sew both pieces next to each other on side opposite of head.

HAMMER

HANDLE

Using green yarn,

R1: Ch 2, 8 sc in second ch from hook.

R2: Sc 2 in each sc around. (16 sts)

R3: *Sc 1, 2 sc in next sc*, rep 8 times. (24 sts)

R4: Through back loops only, *sc 1, dec 1*, rep 8 times. (16 sts)

R5–35: Sc 16, stuffing as you go.

Change to gray,

R36: Sc 16 through back loops only.

R37–43: Sc 16.

Work on face: Position and attach 9 mm eyes; embroider mouth.

PLIERS

Make 2.

Using green yarn,

R1: Ch 2, 6 sc in second ch from hook.

R2: Sc 2 in each sc around. (12 sts)

R3–18: Sc 12, stuffing as you go.

R19: *Sc 1, dec 1*, rep 4 times. (8 sts)

R20 and 21: Sc 8.

Finish stuffing and change to gray yarn. No more stuffing after this!

R22: Sc 8 through back loops only.

R23–33: Sc 8.

R34: Dec 4 times. (4 sts)

Fasten off and weave in end. Position pieces on top of each other and sew together just above green handles. Shape the pliers so they look like the real thing.

OLI'S BABY

I made this baby for Oli right before Martina was born and gave it to her when we got home from the hospital with Marti. Every time (well, not every single time, especially not in the middle of the night!) I'd change Martina's diaper, Oli would change her baby's diaper, and it was the cutest thing to watch. I also cut out rectangular pieces of white felt and put them in an empty wipe container so she had her own wipes! I think Oli's baby would be a nice present for the brother or sister of a new baby. You could also make him a blankie out of little granny squares and bundle him up!

FINISHED SIZE

Approx 9½" tall

MATERIALS

Worsted-weight yarn in desired skin color, and white for diaper and beanie

G/6 (4mm) and 7 (4.5 mm) crochet hooks; use G hook unless otherwise instructed

9 mm plastic eyes with safety backings

Brown and red embroidery floss and tapestry needle

Fiberfill or stuffing of your choice

2 pieces of Velcro with sticky back for diaper

BABY

HEAD

Using skin-colored yarn,

R1: Ch 2, 6 sc in second ch from hook.

R2: Sc 2 in each sc around. (12 sts)

R3: *Sc 1, 2 sc in next sc*, rep 6 times. (18 sts)

R4: *Sc 2, 2 sc in next sc*, rep 6 times. (24 sts)

R5: *Sc 3, 2 sc in next sc*, rep 6 times. (30 sts)

R6: *Sc 4, 2 sc in next sc*, rep 6 times. (36 sts)

R7: *Sc 5, 2 sc in next sc*, rep 6 times. (42 sts)

R8–19: Sc 42.

R20: *Sc 5, dec 1*, rep 6 times. (36 sts)

R21: *Sc 4, dec 1*, rep 6 times. (30 sts)

R22: *Sc 3, dec 1*, rep 6 times. (24 sts)

Work on face: Position and attach eyes; embroider mouth and nose.

R23: Sc 24.

R24: *Sc 2, dec 1*, rep 6 times. (18 sts)

R25: *Sc 1, dec 1*, rep 6 times. (12 sts)

Stuff head.

R26: *Sk 1 sc, sc 1*, rep 6 times. (6 sts)

Fasten off and weave in end.

BODY

Using skin-colored yarn,

R1: Ch 2, 6 sc in second ch from hook.

R2: Sc 2 in each sc around. (12 sts)

R3: *Sc 1, 2 sc in next sc*, rep 6 times. (18 sts)

R4: *Sc 2, 2 sc in next sc*, rep 6 times. (24 sts)

R5: *Sc 3, 2 sc in next sc*, rep 6 times. (30 sts)

R6: *Sc 4, 2 sc in next sc*, rep 6 times. (36 sts)

R7–14: Sc 36.

R15: *Sc 4, dec 1*, rep 6 times. (30 sts)

R16 and 17: Sc 30.

R18: *Sc 3, dec 1*, rep 6 times. (24 sts)

R19 and 20: Sc 24.

Fasten off, leaving long tail for sewing. Stuff and sew to head.

ARMS

Make 2.

Using skin-colored yarn,

R1: Ch 2, 6 sc in second ch from hook.

R2: Sc 2 in each sc around. (12 sts)

R3–23: Sc 12, stuffing as you go.

Fasten off, leaving long tail for sewing. Sew open end tog and sew to body.

LEGS

Make 2.

Using skin-colored yarn,

R1: Ch 2, 6 sc in second ch from hook.

R2: Sc 2 in each sc around. (12 sts)

R3: *Sc 1, 2 sc in next sc*, rep 6 times. (18 sts)

R4: *Sc 2, 2 sc in next sc*, rep 6 times. (24 sts)

R5 and 6: Hdc 12, sc 12.

R7: *Sc 2, dec 1*, rep 6 times. (18 sts)

R8: *Sc 1, dec 1*, rep 6 times. (12 sts)

R9–20: Sc 12, stuffing as you go.

Fasten off, leaving long tail for sewing. Sew to body.

DiaPeR

Using white yarn and working back and forth,

Loosely ch 31.

Row 1: Sc 30, starting in second ch from hook, turn.

Rows 2–7: Ch 1, sc 30, turn.

Row 8: Sl st 10, sc 10, turn.

Row 9: Ch 1, sc 10, turn.

Row 10: Sk 1 sc, sc 7, sk 1 sc, sc 1, turn. (8 sts)

Row 11: Sk 1, sc 5, sk 1 sc, sc 1, turn. (6 sts)

Row 12: Sk 1, sc 3, sk 1 sc, sc 1, turn. (4 sts)

Row 13–16: Ch 1, sc 4, turn.

Row 17: Ch 1, 2 sc in first sc, sc 2, 2 sc in last sc, turn. (6 sts)

Row 18: Ch 1, 2 sc in first sc, sc 4, 2 sc in last sc, turn. (8 sts)

Row 19: Ch 1, 2 sc in first sc, sc 6, 2 sc in last sc, turn. (10 sts)

Row 20: Ch 1, 2 sc in first sc, sc 8, 2 sc in last sc, turn. (12 sts)

Row 21: Ch 1, 2 sc in first sc, sc 10, 2 sc in last sc, turn. (14 sts)

Row 22: Ch 1, 2 sc in first sc, sc 12, 2 sc in last sc, turn. (16 sts)

Rows 23–26: Ch 1, sc 16, turn.

Fasten off and weave in end.

Attach Velcro pieces at each end of WS on longer piece and at each end of RS on shorter piece (see photo at left).

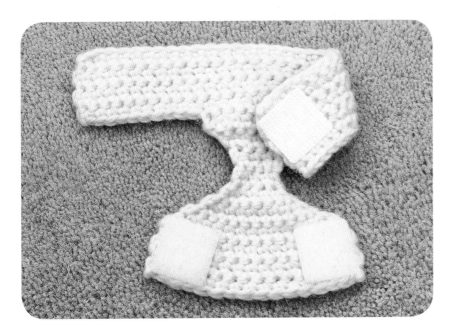

HaT

Using white yarn and a size 7 hook,

R1: Ch 2, 6 sc in second ch from hook.

R2: Sc 2 in each sc around. (12 sts)

R3: *Sc 1, 2 sc in next sc*, rep 6 times. (18 sts)

R4: *Sc 2, 2 sc in next sc*, rep 6 times. (24 sts)

R5: *Sc 3, 2 sc in next sc*, rep 6 times. (30 sts)

R6: *Sc 4, 2 sc in next sc*, rep 6 times. (36 sts)

R7: *Sc 5, 2 sc in next sc*, rep 6 times. (42 sts)

R8–16: Sc 42.

Fasten off and weave in end.

MY FIRST DOLLS

As much as I like the big, real-looking baby dolls, which I bought for Oli when she was one year old, Oli didn't play with hers until she was around four. Both Oli and Martina have always preferred little dolls instead. These would be great for a new baby or a toddler. They're easy to carry around and cuddle with and super fast to make!

If you're making one for a baby or toddler, you could add a rattle or jingle bells to the doll's belly, so it doubles as a rattle.

FINISHED SIZE

Approx 6" tall

MATERIALS

Worsted-weight yarn in desired skin color, orange, blue, green, pink, white, red, and a bit of brown for the hair

F/5 (3.75 mm) crochet hook

9 mm plastic eyes with safety backings

Small pieces of pink craft felt

Sewing thread and sharp needle

Black embroidery floss and tapestry needle

Fiberfill or stuffing of your choice

HEAD

Using skin-colored yarn,

R1: Ch 2, 5 sc in second ch from hook.

R2: Sc 2 in each sc around. (10 sts)

R3: *Sc 1, 2 sc in next sc*, rep 5 times. (15 sts)

R4: *Sc 2, 2 sc in next sc*, rep 5 times. (20 sts)

R5: *Sc 3, 2 sc in next sc*, rep 5 times. (25 sts)

R6: *Sc 4, 2 sc in next sc*, rep 5 times. (30 sts)

R7: *Sc 5, 2 sc in next sc*, rep 5 times. (35 sts)

R8–16: Sc 35.

R17: *Sc 5, dec 1*, rep 5 times. (30 sts)

R18: *Sc 4, dec 1*, rep 5 times. (25 sts)

R19: *Sc 3, dec 1*, rep 5 times. (20 sts)

Work on face: Position and attach eyes; embroider mouth. For cheeks, cut 2 circles from felt and sew to head.

R20: *Sc 2, dec 1*, rep 5 times. (15 sts)

Stuff almost to top.

R21: *Sc 1, dec 1*, rep 5 times. (10 sts)

Finish stuffing.

R22: *Sk 1 sc, sc 1*. (5 sts)

Fasten off and weave in end.

BODY

Using desired yarn color for clothes,

R1: Ch 2, 5 sc in second ch from hook.

R2: Sc 2 in each sc around. (10 sts)

R3: *Sc 1, 2 sc in next sc*, rep 5 times. (15 sts)

R4: *Sc 2, 2 sc in next sc*, rep 5 times. (20 sts)

R5–8: Sc 20.

R9 for boy: Sc 20.

R9 for girl: Sc 20 through back loops only. (You'll use the front loops later when crocheting the skirt.)

R10: Sc 20.

Fasten off, leaving long tail for sewing. Stuff and sew to head.

ARMS AND LEGS

Make 2 of each.

Use skin-colored yarn for arms, use desired yarn color for legs.

R1: Ch 2, 7 sc in second ch from hook.

R2 and 3: Sc 7.

For boy only: Change to yarn color of body for sleeves.

R4: Sc 7, stuffing as you go.

R5–9: Sc 7.

Fasten off, leaving long tail for sewing. Stuff lightly, sew open end of arms tog and sew to body; sew legs to body.

LITTLE SKIRT FOR GIRL

Using white yarn,

Holding doll upside down (legs up in the air), join yarn at back to one of the front loops you left in R9 when making body.

R1: Sc 20 through front loops all around body.

R2: Sc 2 in every sc. (40 sts)

R3 and 4: Sc 40.

Fasten off and weave in end.

HAT FOR BOY

Using the desired yarn color for hat,

R1: Ch 2, 5 sc in second ch from hook.

R2: Sc 2 in each sc around. (10 sts)

R3: *Sc 1, 2 sc in next sc*, rep 5 times. (15 sts)

R4: *Sc 2, 2 sc in next sc*, rep 5 times. (20 sts)

R5: *Sc 3, 2 sc in next sc*, rep 5 times. (25 sts)

R6: *Sc 4, 2 sc in next sc*, rep 5 times. (30 sts)

R7: *Sc 5, 2 sc in next sc*, rep 5 times. (35 sts)

R8–14: Sc 35.

Fasten off and weave in end.

Ear flaps (make 2): Ch 3, dc 6 in third ch from hook. Fasten off, leaving long tail for sewing. Sew flaps to each side of hat where ears would be.

FINISHING

Cut a piece of brown yarn about 8" long. Sew the strand of yarn in and out of the sts at the top of the head to form loops for hair.

Doll cheek

LiTTLe TURTLeS, eGGS, and THeiR MOMMY

Turtles have always been my favorite animals. My very first live turtles were Manuelita and Lucero, and the last one I had in Montevideo was Valentina. We have two little ones now, and again, their names are Manuelita and Lucero. (I'm so original!) I just had to make turtles for this second book, and it made sense to make them into some kind of game. You can count the eggs that are in the turtle's "belly," count the baby turtles that were born, and the best part for us parents? They can all be stored inside the turtle, so no eggs or babies will be lost under the beds, the couch, or wherever lost things go to live after they leave our houses.

FiNiSHeD SiZeS

Mommy Turtle: Approx 3" tall and 7" long

Little Turtles: Approx 1½" tall

Eggs: Approx 2" tall

MaTeRiaLS

Worsted-weight yarn in green, brown, orange, and white

G/6 (4 mm) crochet hook

6 mm and 9 mm plastic eyes with safety backings

Tapestry needle

Fiberfill or stuffing of your choice

MOMMY TURTLe

SHeLL TOP

Using brown yarn,

R1: Ch 2, 6 sc in second ch from hook.

R2: Sc 2 in each sc around. (12 sts)

R3: *Sc 1, 2 sc in next sc*, rep 6 times. (18 sts)

R4: *Sc 2, 2 sc in next sc*, rep 6 times. (24 sts)

R5: *Sc 3, 2 sc in next sc*, rep 6 times. (30 sts)

R6: *Sc 4, 2 sc in next sc*, rep 6 times. (36 sts)

R7: *Sc 5, 2 sc in next sc*, rep 6 times. (42 sts)

R8: *Sc 6, 2 sc in next sc*, rep 6 times. (48 sts)

R9: *Sc 7, 2 sc in next sc*, rep 6 times. (54 sts)

R10: *Sc 8, 2 sc in next sc*, rep 6 times. (60 sts)

R11: *Sc 9, 2 sc in next sc*, rep 6 times. (66 sts)

R12: *Sc 10, 2 sc in next sc*, rep 6 times. (72 sts)

R13–23: Sc 72.

R24: Sc 72 through back loops only.

Fasten off and weave in end. To create segments on the shell, using orange yarn, backstitch (page 78) embroider three horizontal lines around the shell, working the first one between the 7th and 8th row from the center at the top of the shell. Embroider the second line 7 rows from the first one, and the third line 7 rows from the second one. Then divide the horizontal circles into 4 equal segments and embroider 4 vertical lines between the circles, offsetting the lines between circles as shown.

SHELL BOTTOM

Using orange yarn,

R1: Ch 2, 6 sc in second ch from hook.

R2: Sc 2 in each sc around. (12 sts)

R3: *Sc 1, 2 sc in next sc*, rep 6 times. (18 sts)

R4: *Sc 2, 2 sc in next sc*, rep 6 times. (24 sts)

R5: *Sc 3, 2 sc in next sc*, rep 6 times. (30 sts)

R6: *Sc 4, 2 sc in next sc*, rep 6 times. (36 sts)

R7: *Sc 5, 2 sc in next sc*, rep 6 times. (42 sts)

R8: *Sc 6, 2 sc in next sc*, rep 6 times. (48 sts)

R9: *Sc 7, 2 sc in next sc*, rep 6 times. (54 sts)

R10: *Sc 8, 2 sc in next sc*, rep 6 times. (60 sts)

R11: *Sc 9, 2 sc in next sc*, rep 6 times. (66 sts)

R12: *Sc 10, 2 sc in next sc*, rep 6 times. (72 sts)

R13 and 14: Sc 72.

Fasten off and weave in end.

HEAD

Using green yarn,

R1: Ch 2, 5 sc in second ch from hook.

R2: Sc 2 in each sc around. (10 sts)

R3: *Sc 1, 2 sc in next sc*, rep 5 times. (15 sts)

R4: *Sc 2, 2 sc in next sc*, rep 5 times. (20 sts)

R5: Sc 20.

R6: *Sc 3, 2 sc in next sc*, rep 5 times. (25 sts)

R7–11: Sc 25.

Work on face: Position and attach 9 mm eyes.

R12: *Sc 3, dec 1*, rep 5 times. (20 sts)

R13–19: Sc 20.

Fasten off, leaving long tail for sewing. Stuff firmly, sew open end tog, and sew to shell bottom. (Make sure right side of shell is facing down when you sew head and legs).

FRONT LEGS

Make 2.

Using green yarn,

R1: Ch 2, 5 sc in second ch from hook.

R2: Sc 2 in each sc around. (10 sts)

R3: Sc 10.

R4: *Sc 1, 2 sc in next sc*, rep 5 times. (15 sts)

R5–12: Sc 15.

R13–15: Hdc 8 in front loops only, sc 7.

R16–19: Sc 15.

Fasten off, leaving long tail for sewing. Stuff lightly, sew open end tog, and sew to shell bottom.

BACK LEGS

Make 2.

Using green yarn,

R1: Ch 2, 5 sc in second ch from hook.

R2: Sc 2 in each sc around. (10 sts)

R3: Sc 10.

R4: *Sc 1, 2 sc in next sc*, rep 5 times. (15 sts)

R5–15: Sc 15.

Fasten off, leaving long tail for sewing. Stuff lightly, sew open end tog, and sew to shell bottom.

FINISHING

Align sts of shell top with sts of shell bottom and sew tog, leaving an opening between back legs big enough to fit one of the eggs.

Using brown yarn, join yarn to one of front sts you left in R24 of shell top.

R1: Sc 72.

R2 and 3: Hdc 72.

Fasten off and weave in end.

LITTLE TURTLE

Make 2.

SHELL TOP

Using brown yarn,

R1: Ch 2, 6 sc in second ch from hook.

R2: Sc 2 in each sc around. (12 sts)

R3: *Sc 1, 2 sc in next sc*, rep 6 times. (18 sts)

R4–6: Sc 18.

R7: Sc 18 through back loops only.

Fasten off and weave in end.

SHELL BOTTOM

Using brown yarn,

R1: Ch 2, 6 sc in second ch from hook.

R2: Sc 2 in each sc around. (12 sts)

R3: *Sc 1, 2 sc in next sc*, rep 6 times. (18 sts)

Fasten off, leaving long tail for sewing.

HEAD

Using green yarn,

R1: Ch 2, 5 sc in second ch from hook.

R2: Sc 2 in each sc around. (10 sts)

R3: *Sc 1, 2 sc in next sc*, rep 5 times. (15 sts)

R4 and 5: Sc 15.

Work on face: Position and attach 6 mm eyes.

R6: *Sc 1, dec 1*, rep 5 times. (10 sts)

Fasten off, leaving long tail for sewing. Stuff head and sew to shell top, above R7.

LEGS

Make 4.

Using green yarn,

R1: Ch 2, 5 sc in second ch from hook.

R2–4: Sc 5.

Fasten off, leaving long tail for sewing. Sew open end tog and sew to shell bottom.

FINISHING

Align sts of shell top with sts of shell bottom and sew around.

Using brown yarn, join yarn to one of front sts you left in R7 of shell top.

R1: Sc 18.

R2: Sc 18.

Fasten off and weave in end.

EGGS

WHOLE EGG

Make 4.

Using white yarn,

R1: Ch 2, 5 sc in second ch from hook.

R2: Sc 2 in each sc around. (10 sts)

R3: *Sc 1, 2 sc in next sc*, rep 5 times. (15 sts)

R4: *Sc 2, 2 sc in next sc*, rep 5 times. (20 sts)

R5: *Sc 3, 2 sc in next sc*, rep 5 times. (25 sts)

R6–12: Sc 25.

R13: *Sc 3, dec 1*, rep 5 times. (20 sts)

R14: *Sc 2, dec 1*, rep 5 times. (15 sts)

Stuff lightly.

R15: *Sc 1, dec 1*, rep 5 times. (10 sts)

R16: *Sk 1 sc, sc 1*, rep 5 times. (5 sts)

Fasten off and weave in end.

CRACKED EGG

Make 1.

Using white yarn,

R1: Ch 2, 5 sc in second ch from hook.

R2: Sc 2 in each sc around. (10 sts)

R3: *Sc 1, 2 sc in next sc*, rep 5 times. (15 sts)

R4: *Sc 2, 2 sc in next sc*, rep 5 times. (20 sts)

R5: *Sc 3, 2 sc in next sc*, rep 5 times. (25 sts)

R6–10: Sc 25.

R11: * Sl st 1, hdc 2, dc 2*, rep 4 more times.

Fasten off and weave in end.

LITTLE FISH AND HER DADDY

Martina has always liked fish. As a tiny little newborn, she would stare at my computer screen saver, full of colorful fishes swimming around, and now she loves to go to the pet store and spend time with her head stuck to the huge fish tanks!

I made her these a while ago, and she still plays with them often. Make a huge school of colorful fishes for your favorite fish lover and let them pretend to swim together.

FINISHED SIZES

Daddy Fish: Approx 7" long
Little Fish: Approx 5" long

MATERIALS

Worsted-weight yarn in blue, green, red, and orange

G/6 (4 mm) crochet hook

9 mm plastic eyes with safety backings

Black embroidery floss and tapestry needle

Fiberfill or stuffing of your choice

DADDY FISH

EYE ROUNDIES

Make 2.

Using blue yarn,

R1: Ch 2, 6 sc in second ch from hook.

R2: Sc 2 in each sc around. (12 sts)

Fasten off, leaving long tail for sewing, set aside.

BODY

Using green yarn,

R1: Ch 2, 6 sc in second ch from hook.

R2: Sc 2 in each sc around. (12 sts)

R3: Sc 12.

R4: *Sc 1, 2 sc in next sc*, rep 6 times. (18 sts)

R5: Sc 18.

R6: *Sc 2, 2 sc in next sc*, rep 6 times. (24 sts)

R7: Sc 24.

R8: *Sc 3, 2 sc in next sc*, rep 6 times. (30 sts)

R9: Sc 30.

R10: *Sc 4, 2 sc in next sc*, rep 6 times. (36 sts)

R11–13: Sc 36.

Work on face: Put plastic eyes through eye roundies, attach eyes to head, sew roundies to head, and embroider mouth.

Change to blue yarn and alternate 1 blue rnd and 1 green rnd to end of body.

R14–24: Sc 36.

R25: *Sc 4, dec 1*, rep 6 times. (30 sts)

R26: *Sc 3, dec 1*, rep 6 times. (24 sts)

R27: *Sc 2, dec 1*, rep 6 times. (18 sts)

R28: Sc 18.

Stuff almost to top.

R29: *Sc 1, dec 1*, rep 6 times. (12 sts)

R30: Sc 12.

Finish stuffing.

R31: *Sk 1 sc, sc 1*, rep 6 times. (6 sts)

Fasten off and weave in end.

TOP FIN

Using blue yarn,

R1: Ch 2, 8 sc in second ch from hook.

R2: Sc 2 in each sc around. (16 sts)

R3–5: Sc 16.

Fasten off, leaving long tail for sewing. Sew to top of body.

SIDE FIN

Make 2.

Using blue yarn,

R1: Ch 2, 6 sc in second ch from hook.

R2: Sc 2 in each sc around. (12 sts)

R3: *Sc 1, 2 sc in next sc*, rep 6 times. (18 sts)

R4–6: Sc 18.

R7: *Sc 1, dec 1*, rep 6 times. (12 sts)

R8: *Sk 1 sc, sc 1*, rep 6 times. (6 sts)

R9 and 10: Sc 6.

Fasten off, leaving long tail for sewing. Sew to side of body.

TAIL

Make 2.

Using blue yarn,

R1: Ch 2, 6 sc in second ch from hook.

R2: Sc 6.

R3: Sc 2 in each sc around. (12 sts)

R4: Sc 12.

R5: *Sc 1, 2 sc in next sc*, rep 6 times. (18 sts)

R6: Sc 18.

R7: *Sc 2, 2 sc in next sc*, rep 6 times. (24 sts)

R8–12: Sc 24.

R13: *Sc 2, dec 1*, rep 6 times. (18 sts)

R14: Sc 18.

R15: *Sc 1, dec 1*, rep 6 times. (12 sts)

R16: Sc 12.

R17: *Sk 1 sc, sc 1*, rep 6 times. (6 sts)

Fasten off, leaving long tail for sewing. Sew 2 tails next to each other at end of body.

BOTTOM FIN

Using blue yarn,

R1: Ch 2, 5 sc in second ch from hook.

R2: Sc 2 in each sc around. (10 sts)

R3 and 4: Sc 10.

Fasten off, leaving long tail for sewing, and sew to bottom of fish.

LiTTLe FiSH

EYE ROUNDIES

Make 2.

Using red yarn,

R1: Ch 2, 6 sc in second ch from hook.

R2: Sc 2 in each sc around. (12 sts)

Fasten off, leaving long tail for sewing, set aside.

BODY

Using orange yarn,

R1: Ch 2, 6 sc in second ch from hook.

R2: Sc 2 in each sc around. (12 sts)

R3: Sc 12.

R4: *Sc 1, 2 sc in next sc*, rep 6 times. (18 sts)

R5: Sc 18.

R6: *Sc 2, 2 sc in next sc*, rep 6 times. (24 sts)

R7–11: Sc 24.

Work on face: Put plastic eyes through eye roundies, attach eyes to head, sew roundies to head, and embroider mouth.

Change to red yarn and alternate 1 red rnd and 1 orange rnd to end of body.

R12–16: Sc 24.

R17: *Sc 2, dec 1*, rep 6 times. (18 sts)

R18: Sc 18.

Stuff almost to top.

R19: *Sc 1, dec 1*, rep 6 times. (12 sts)

R20: Sc 12.

Finish stuffing.

R21: *Sk 1 sc, sc 1*, rep 6 times. (6 sts)

Fasten off and weave in end.

TOP FIN

Using red yarn,

R1: Ch 2, 6 sc in second ch from hook.

R2: Sc 2 in each sc around. (12 sts)

R3 and 4: Sc 12.

Fasten off, leaving long tail for sewing. Sew to top of body.

SIDE FIN

Make 2.

Using red yarn,

R1: Ch 2, 6 sc in second ch from hook.

R2: Sc 2 in each sc around. (12 sts)

R3–6: Sc 12.

R7: *Sk 1 sc, sc 1*, rep 6 times. (6 sts)

R8: Sc 6.

Fasten off, leaving long tail for sewing. Sew to side of body.

TAIL

Make 2.

Using red yarn,

R1: Ch 2, 6 sc in second ch from hook.

R2: Sc 6.

R3: Sc 2 in each sc around. (12 sts)

R4: Sc 12.

R5: *Sc 1, 2 sc in next sc*, rep 6 times. (18 sts)

R6–8: Sc 18.

R9: *Sc 1, dec 1*, rep 6 times. (12 sts)

R10: Sc 12.

R11: Sk 1 sc, sc 1. (6 sts)

Fasten off, leaving long tail for sewing. Sew 2 tails next to each other at end of body.

BOTTOM FIN

Using red yarn,

R1: Ch 2, 6 sc in second ch from hook.

R2 and 3: Sc 6.

Fasten off, leaving long tail for sewing, and sew to bottom of body.

LITTLE SQUIRREL AND HER MOMMY

When I was pregnant with Oli, I had a scary dream about squirrels trying to attack me and take her from my belly! I've been terrified of squirrels ever since. (I know it's dumb, but I can't help it.) Oli thinks it's the funniest story and loves to tell it to random people in the street when we go out to walk Santiago, our dog. You should see their faces—they probably think I'm nuts! I made these squirrels to get over the phobia (I figured it'd be some kind of yarn therapy), and while it didn't work at all, I'm really happy with how they turned out. I hope you like them too!

FINISHED SIZES
Mommy Squirrel: Approx 5½" tall
Little Squirrel: Approx 4½" tall

MATERIALS
Worsted-weight yarn in tan, brown, red, and white

G/6 (4 mm) crochet hook

12 mm plastic eyes with safety backings

Small pieces of tan and white craft felt

Sewing thread and sharp needle

Brown embroidery floss and tapestry needle

Fiberfill or stuffing of your choice

MOMMY SQUIRREL

HEAD

Using tan yarn,

R1: Ch 2, 6 sc in second ch from hook.

R2: Sc 2 in each sc around. (12 sts)

R3: *Sc 1, 2 sc in next sc*, rep 6 times. (18 sts)

R4: *Sc 2, 2 sc in next sc*, rep 6 times. (24 sts)

R5: *Sc 3, 2 sc in next sc*, rep 6 times. (30 sts)

R6: *Sc 4, 2 sc in next sc*, rep 6 times. (36 sts)

R7–17: Sc 36.

R18: *Sc 4, dec 1*, rep 6 times. (30 sts)

R19: *Sc 3, dec 1*, rep 6 times. (24 sts)

Work on face: Position and attach eyes, cut a piece of tan felt, embroider mouth and nose, and sew to head.

R20: *Sc 2, dec 1*, rep 6 times. (18 sts)
Stuff firmly.

R21: *Sc 1, dec 1*, rep 6 times. (12 sts)
Finish stuffing.

R22: *Sk 1 sc, sc 1*, rep 6 times. (6 sts)
Fasten off and weave in end.

EARS

Make 2.

Using tan yarn,

R1: Ch 2, 5 sc in second ch from hook.

R2: Sc 5.

R3: Sc 2 in each sc around. (10 sts)

R4 and 5: Sc 10.

Fasten off, leaving long tail for sewing. Sew to head.

BODY

Using tan yarn,

R1: Ch 2, 6 sc in second ch from hook.

R2: Sc 2 sc in each sc around. (12 sts)

R3: *Sc 1, 2 sc in next sc*, rep 6 times. (18 sts)

R4: *Sc 2, 2 sc in next sc*, rep 6 times. (24 sts)

R5–13: Sc 24.

Fasten off, leaving long tail for sewing. Stuff and sew to head.

ARMS

Make 2.

Using tan yarn,

R1: Ch 2, 5 sc in second ch from hook.

R2: Sc 2 in each sc around. (10 sts)

R3–8: Sc 10.

Fasten off, leaving long tail for sewing. Sew open end tog and sew to body (I didn't stuff them).

LEGS

Make 2.

Using brown yarn,

R1: Ch 2, 5 sc in second ch from hook.

R2: Sc 2 in each sc around. (10 sts)

R3–11: Sc 10.

Fasten off, leaving long tail for sewing. Stuff, sew open end tog and set aside.

TAIL

Using brown yarn,

R1: Ch 2, 6 sc in second ch from hook.

R2: Sc 2 in each sc around. (12 sts)

R3: *Sc 1, 2 sc in next sc*, rep 6 times. (18 sts)

R4: *Sc 2, 2 sc in next sc*, rep 6 times. (24 sts)

R5: *Sc 3, 2 sc in next sc*, rep 6 times. (30 sts)

R6–13: Sc 30.

R14: *Sc 3, dec 1*, rep 6 times. (24 sts)

R15–21: Sc 24.

R22: *Sc 2, dec 1*, rep 6 times. (18 sts)

R23–32: Sc 18.

Fasten off, leaving long tail for sewing. Stuff lightly near the top, sew open end tog, and sew bottom of tail

between legs. Then sew bottom of tail/leg unit to bottom of body around inside of legs and tail. Sew top of tail to back of head to keep tail upright.

Sew bottom of tail between legs.

Sew legs and tail to body.

MUSHROOM

TOP

Using red yarn,

R1: Ch 2, 6 sc in second ch from hook.

R2: Sc 2 in each sc around. (12 sts)

R3: *Sc 1, 2 sc in next sc*, rep 6 times. (18 sts)

R4: *Sc 2, 2 sc in next sc*, rep 6 times. (24 sts)

R5–9: Sc 24.

R10: *Sc 2, dec 1*, rep 6 times. (18 sts)

Sew a round white felt dot to mushroom.

R11: *Sc 1, dec 1*, rep 6 times. (12 sts)

Stuff.

R12: *Sk 1 sc, sc 1*, rep 6 times. (6 sts)

Fasten off and weave in end.

STEM

Using white yarn,

R1: Ch 2, 6 sc in second ch from hook.

R2: Sc 2 in each sc around. (12 sts)

R3: Sc 12.

Fasten off, leaving long tail for sewing. Stuff and sew to top of mushroom.

Sew mushroom between mommy squirrel's arms.

LITTLE SQUIRREL

HEAD

Using tan yarn,

R1: Ch 2, 6 sc in second ch from hook.

R2: Sc 2 in each sc around. (12 sts)

R3: *Sc 1, 2 sc in next sc*, rep 6 times. (18 sts)

R4: *Sc 2, 2 sc in next sc*, rep 6 times. (24 sts)

R5: *Sc 3, 2 sc in next sc*, rep 6 times. (30 sts)

R6–14: Sc 30.

R15: *Sc 3, dec 1*, rep 6 times. (24 sts)

Work on face: Position and attach eyes, cut a little piece of tan felt, embroider mouth and nose, and sew to face.

16: Sc 18.

: *Sc 1, dec 1*, rep 6 times. (12 sts)

and 19: Sc 12.

en off, leaving long tail for sewing.
tuff tail lightly, sew open end tog,
nd sew to body.

2.

brown yarn,

2, 6 sc in second ch from hook.

Sc 6.

off, leaving long tail for sewing.
w open end tog and sew to body.

**Mommy squirrel
muzzle**

**Little squirrel
muzzle**

M
U
R
R

Fasten off, leaving long tail for sewing.
   Sew open end tog and sew to body.

TAIL

Using brown yarn,

R1: Ch 2, 6 sc in second ch from hook.

R2: Sc 2 in each sc around. (12 sts)

R3: *Sc 1, 2 sc in next sc*, rep 6 times.
   (18 sts)

LITTLE TIGER AND HER MOMMY

When Oli was little, her favorite book was I Don't Want to Go to Bed! *by Julie Sykes and Tim Warnes, a story of a little tiger that doesn't want to go to sleep. So for a while she wanted tiger everything—tiger shirts, tiger books, and tiger toys! Here is my version of Little Tiger and her mom! Hope your little tiger likes it too.*

FINISHED SIZES

Mommy Tiger: Approx 9" tall
Little Tiger: Approx 7" tall

MATERIALS

Worsted-weight yarn in orange, black, and white

G/6 (4 mm) crochet hook

9 mm plastic eyes with safety backings

Black embroidery floss and tapestry needle

Fiberfill or stuffing of your choice

MOMMY TIGER

MUZZLE

Using white yarn,

R1: Ch 2, 6 sc in second ch from hook.

R2: Sc 2 in each sc around. (12 sts)

R3: *Sc 1, 2 sc in next sc*, rep 6 times. (18 sts)

R4 and 5: Sc 18.

Fasten off, leaving long tail for sewing. Embroider nose and mouth; set aside.

HEAD

Using orange yarn,

R1: Ch 2, 6 sc in second ch from hook.

R2: Sc 2 in each sc around. (12 sts)

R3: *Sc 1, 2 sc in next sc*, rep 6 times. (18 sts)

R4: *Sc 2, 2 sc in next sc*, rep 6 times. (24 sts)

R5: *Sc 3, 2 sc in next sc*, rep 6 times. (30 sts)

R6: *Sc 4, 2 sc in next sc*, rep 6 times. (36 sts)

R7: *Sc 5, 2 sc in next sc*, rep 6 times. (42 sts)

R8–19: Sc 42.

R20: *Sc 5, dec 1*, rep 6 times. (36 sts)

R21: *Sc 4, dec 1*, rep 6 times. (30 sts)

R22: *Sc 3, dec 1*, rep 6 times. (24 sts)

Work on face: Position and attach eyes; sew muzzle in place.

R23: *Sc 2, dec 1*, rep 6 times. (18 sts)

R24: Sc 18.

Stuff head firmly.

R25: *Sc 1, dec 1*, rep 6 times. (12 sts)

Fasten off and weave in end.

EARS

Make 2.

Using orange yarn,

R1: Ch 2, 6 sc in second ch from hook.

R2: Sc 6.

R3: Sc 2 in each sc around. (12 sts)

R4: Sc 12.

Fasten off, leaving long tail for sewing. Sew to head.

HEAD STRIPES

Use black yarn for all stripes.

Stripes A at top of head

Make 2.

Loosely ch 13. Beg at second ch from hook, sl st 1, sc 2, hdc 2, dc 2, hdc 2, sc 2, sl st 1.

Fasten off, leaving long tail for sewing. Sew to top of head.

Stripe B at back of head

Loosely ch 16. Beg at second ch from hook, sl st 1, sc 2, hdc 2, dc 5, hdc 2, sc 2, sl st 1.

Fasten off, leaving long tail for sewing. Sew at back of head below A stripes.

Stripe C at back of head

Loosely ch 19. Beg at second ch from hook, sl st 1, sc 2, hdc 2, dc 8, hdc 2, sc 2, sl st 1.

Fasten off, leaving long tail for sewing. Sew at back of head below B stripe.

Stripes on cheeks

Make 4.

Loosely ch 9. Beg at second ch from hook, sl st 1, sc 2, hdc 2, sc 2, sl st 1.

Fasten off, leaving long tail for sewing. Sew to face.

BODY

Using orange yarn,

R1: Ch 2, 6 sc in second ch from hook.

R2: Sc 2 in each sc around. (12 sts)

R3: *Sc 1, 2 sc in next sc*, rep 6 times. (18 sts)

R4: *Sc 2, 2 sc in next sc*, rep 6 times. (24 sts)

R5: *Sc 3, 2 sc in next sc*, rep 6 times. (30 sts)

R6: *Sc 4, 2 sc in next sc*, rep 6 times. (36 sts)

R7–14: Sc 36.

R15: *Sc 4, dec 1*, rep 6 times. (30 sts)

R16–19: Sc 30.

Fasten off, leaving long tail for sewing. Stuff firmly and sew to head.

BODY STRIPES

Make 3.

Using black yarn,

Loosely ch 33.

Beg at second ch from hook: Sl st 1, sc 2, hdc 2, dc 22, hdc 2, sc 2, sl st 1.

Fasten off, leaving long tail for sewing. Sew around body.

LEGS AND ARMS

Make 4.

Using orange yarn,

R1: Ch 2, 7 sc in second ch from hook.

R2: Sc 2 in each sc around. (14 sts)

R3–15: Sc 14.

Fasten off, leaving long tail for sewing. Stuff, sew open end of arms tog, and sew to body; sew legs to body.

TAIL

Using orange yarn,

R1: Ch 2, 6 sc in second ch from hook.

R2: Sc 6.

Rep R2 until tail is approx 4"/10 cm long.

Fasten off, leaving tail for sewing. Sew open end tog and sew to body.

Little Tiger

MUZZLE

Using white yarn,

R1: Ch 2, 6 sc in second ch from hook.

R2: Sc 2 in each sc around. (12 sts)

R3 and 4: Sc 12.

Fasten off, leaving long tail for sewing. Embroider nose and mouth, set aside.

HEAD

Using orange yarn,

R1: Ch 2, 6 sc in second ch from hook.

R2: Sc 2 in each sc around. (12 sts)

R3: *Sc 1, 2 sc in next sc*, rep 6 times. (18 sts)

R4: *Sc 2, 2 sc in next sc*, rep 6 times. (24 sts)

R5: *Sc 3, 2 sc in next sc*, rep 6 times. (30 sts)

R6: *Sc 4, 2 sc in next sc*, rep 6 times. (36 sts)

R7–17: Sc 36.

R18: *Sc 4, dec 1*, rep 6 times. (30 sts)

R19: *Sc 3, dec 1*, rep 6 times. (24 sts)

Work on face: Position and attach eyes, sew muzzle in place.

R20: *Sc 2, dec 1*, rep 6 times. (18 sts)

R21: Sc 18.

R22: *Sc 1, dec 1*, rep 6 times. (12 sts)

Stuff head firmly.

R23: *Sk 1 sc, sc 1*, rep 6 times. (6 sts)

Fasten off and weave in end.

EARS

Make 2.

Using orange yarn,

R1: Ch 2, 6 sc in second ch from hook.

R2: Sc 6.

R3: Sc 2 in each sc around. (12 sts)

R4: Sc 12.

Fasten off, leaving long tail for sewing. Sew to head.

HEAD STRIPES

Use black yarn for all stripes.

Stripes A at top of head

Make 2.

Loosely ch 10. Beg at second ch from hook, sl st 1, sc 2, hdc 3, sc 2, sl st 1.

Fasten off, leaving long tail for sewing. Sew to top of head.

Stripes B at back of head

Make 2.

Loosely ch 15. Beg at second ch from hook, sl st 1, sc 2, hdc 8, sc 2, sl st 1.

Fasten off, leaving long tail for sewing. Sew to back of head below A stripes.

Stripes on cheeks

Make 2.

Loosely ch 9. Beg at second ch from hook, sl st 1, sc 2, hdc 2, sc 2, sl st 1.

Fasten off, leaving long tail for sewing. Sew to face.

BODY

Using orange yarn,

R1: Ch 2, 6 sc in second ch from hook.

R2: Sc 2 in each sc around. (12 sts)

R3: *Sc 1, 2 sc in next sc*, rep 6 times. (18 sts)

R4: *Sc 2, 2 sc in next sc*, rep 6 times. (24 sts)

R5: *Sc 3, 2 sc in next sc*, rep 6 times. (30 sts)

R6–12: Sc 30.

R13: *Sc 3, dec 1*, rep 6 times. (24 sts)

R14–16: Sc 24.

Fasten off, leaving long tail for sewing. Stuff firmly and sew to head.

BODY STRIPES

Make 2.

Using black yarn, loosely ch 29. Beg at second ch from hook, sl st 1, sc 2, hdc 22, sc 2, sl st 1.

Fasten off, leaving long tail for sewing. Sew around body.

LEGS AND ARMS

Make 4.

Using orange yarn,

R1: Ch 2, 6 sc in second ch from hook.

R2: Sc 2 in each sc around. (12 sts)

R3–12: Sc 12.

Fasten off, leaving long tail for sewing. Stuff, sew open end tog, and sew to body.

TAIL

Using orange yarn,

R1: Ch 2, 4 sc in second ch from hook.

R2: Sc 4.

Rep R2 until tail is approx 3"/7 cm long.

Fasten off, leaving a tail for sewing. Sew open end tog and sew to body.

LITTLE BEE AND HER MOMMY

Bee Movie! Seinfeld! We just had to see it, and you know how it goes . . . I just had to make some bees. Make a few more baby bees and hang them from the Branch Mobile or use them in a Stroller Toy; I bet you they'd look really cute!

FINISHED SIZES
Mommy Bee: Approx 5½" tall
Little Bee: Approx 4" tall

MATERIALS
Worsted-weight yarn in white, yellow, and black

G/6 (4 mm) crochet hook

9 mm plastic eyes with safety backings

Black embroidery floss and tapestry needle

Fiberfill or stuffing of your choice

MOMMY BEE

HEAD

Using black yarn,

R1: Ch 2, sc 6 in second ch from hook.

R2: Sc 2 in each sc around. (12 sts)

R3: *Sc 1, 2 sc in next sc*, rep 6 times. (18 sts)

R4: *Sc 2, 2 sc in next sc*, rep 6 times. (24 sts)

R5: *Sc 3, 2 sc in next sc*, rep 6 times. (30 sts)

R6: *Sc 4, 2 sc in next sc*, rep 6 times. (36 sts)

R7 and 8: Sc 36.

Change to yellow,

R9–15: Sc 36.

R16: *Sc 4, dec 1*, rep 6 times. (30 sts)

R17: Sc 30.

Work on face: Position and attach eyes; embroider mouth.

R18: *Sc 3, dec 1*, rep 6 times. (24 sts)

R19: *Sc 2, dec 1*, rep 6 times. (18 sts)

R20: *Sc 1, dec 1*, rep 6 times. (12 sts)

Stuff head.

R21: *Sk 1 sc, sc 1*, rep 6 times. (6 sts)

Fasten off and weave in end.

BODY

Starting with black yarn, alternate 1 rnd yellow and 1 rnd black to end of body.

R1: Ch 2, sc 6 in second ch from hook.

R2: Sc 6.

R3: Sc 2 in each sc around. (12 sts)

R4: Sc 12.

R5: *Sc 1, 2 sc in next sc*, rep 6 times. (18 sts)

R6: Sc 18.

R7: *Sc 2, 2 sc in next sc*, rep 6 times. (24 sts)

R8–15: Sc 24.

Fasten off, leaving long tail for sewing. Stuff and sew to head.

WINGS

Make 4.

Using white yarn,

R1: Ch 2, sc 6 in second ch from hook.

R2: Sc 2 in each sc around. (12 sts)

R3–9: Sc 12.

R10: Dec 6 times. (6 sts)

R11: Sc 6.

Fasten off, leaving long tail for sewing. Sew open end tog and sew 2 wings to each side of body.

LITTLE BEE

HEAD

Using black yarn,

R1: Ch 2, sc 6 in second ch from hook.

R2: Sc 2 in each sc around. (12 sts)

R3: *Sc 1, 2 sc in next sc*, rep 6 times. (18 sts)

R4: *Sc 2, 2 sc in next sc*, rep 6 times. (24 sts)

R5: *Sc 3, 2 sc in next sc*, rep 6 times. (30 sts)

R6 and 7: Sc 30.

Change to yellow,

R8–13: Sc 30.

R14: *Sc 3, dec 1*, rep 6 times. (24 sts)

R15: Sc 24.

Work on face: Position and attach eyes, embroider mouth.

R16: *Sc 2, dec 1*, rep 6 times. (18 sts)

R17: *Sc 1, dec 1*, rep 6 times. (12 sts)

Stuff head.

R18: *Sk 1 sc, sc 1*, rep 6 times. (6 sts)

Fasten off and weave in end.

BODY

Starting with black yarn, alternate 1 rnd yellow and 1 rnd black to end of body.

R1: Ch 2, sc 6 in second ch from hook.

R2: Sc 6.

R3: Sc 2 in each sc around. (12 sts)

R4: Sc 12.

R5: *Sc 1, 2 sc in next sc*, rep 6 times. (18 sts)

R6–11: Sc 18.

Fasten off, leaving long tail for sewing. Stuff and sew to head.

WINGS

Make 4.

Using white yarn,

R1: Ch 2, sc 5 in second ch from hook.

R2: Sc 2 in each sc around. (10 sts)

R3–6: Sc 10.

R7: Dec 5 times. (5 sts)

R8: Sc 5.

Fasten off, leaving long tail for sewing. Sew open end tog and sew 2 wings to each side of body.

FINISHING

Antennae: For mommy, join black yarn to one side of head in first row of black above yellow. Ch 6, fasten off, and weave in end. Rep on other side. For little bee, repeat as for mommy but ch 4 instead of 6.

BOY aND GiRL ROBOTS

Once in a while Oli and Martina like to pretend they're robots. The funniest part is the talking—even they think it's funny and giggle like crazy while asking for cookies and trying to walk like they're covered in cement! This is a really easy pattern, and you could customize it and add more "lights" here and there and even some shiny sequins to make your kid's favorite little robot.

FiNiSHED SiZES

Boy: Approx 8" tall

Girl: Approx 8" tall

MaTERiaLS

Worsted-weight yarn in gray, blue, green, yellow, pink, red, and white

G/6 (4 mm) crochet hook

15 mm plastic eyes with safety backings

Black and red embroidery floss and tapestry needle

Fiberfill or stuffing of your choice

BODY

Using gray yarn,

R1: Ch 2, 5 sc in second ch from hook.

R2: Sc 2 in each sc around. (10 sts)

R3: *Sc 1, 2 sc in next sc*, rep 5 times. (15 sts)

R4: *Sc 2, 2 sc in next sc*, rep 5 times. (20 sts)

R5: *Sc 3, 2 sc in next sc*, rep 5 times. (25 sts)

R6: *Sc 4, 2 sc in next sc*, rep 5 times. (30 sts)

R7: *Sc 5, 2 sc in next sc*, rep 5 times. (35 sts)

R8: *Sc 6, 2 sc in next sc*, rep 5 times. (40 sts)

R9–17: Sc 40.

Work on face: Position and attach eyes, embroider mouth.

Change to green or pink yarn.

R18–20: Sc 40.

Change to blue or red yarn.

R21–25: Sc 40.

Change to green or pink yarn.

R26–28: Sc 40.

Change to blue or red yarn.

R29: Sc 40 through back loops only.

R30: *Sc 6, dec 1*, rep 5 times. (35 sts)

R31: *Sc 5, dec 1*, rep 5 times. (30 sts)

R32: *Sc 4, dec 1*, rep 5 times. (25 sts)

Stuff almost to the top.

R33: *Sc 3, dec 1*, rep 5 times. (20 sts)

R34: *Sc 2, dec 1*, rep 5 times. (15 sts)

Finish stuffing.

R35: *Sc 1, dec 1*, rep 5 times. (10 sts)

R36: Dec 5 times. (5 sts)

Fasten off, leaving long tail to close up the little hole.

aNTENNa

Make 1 for boy; make 2 for girl.

STEM

Using gray yarn,

R1: Ch 2, sc 4 in second ch from hook.

R2–4: Sc 4.

Fasten off, leaving long tail for sewing, set aside.

LIGHT

Using yellow or white yarn,

R1: Ch 2, 6 sc in second ch from hook.

R2: Sc 2 in each sc around. (12 sts)

R3–6: Sc 12.

Stuff.

R7: Dec 6 times. (6 sts)

Fasten off, leaving long tail for sewing. Sew to end of stem. Sew 1 antenna to top of boy's head, and sew 2 antennae to sides of girl's head.

ARMS

LIGHT AT TOP OF ARM

Make 2.

Using yellow or white yarn,

R1: Ch 2, 5 sc in second ch from hook.

R2: Sc 2 in each sc around. (10 sts)

R3: *Sc 1, 2 sc in next sc*, rep 5 times. (15 sts)

R4–7: Sc 15.

Fasten off, leaving long tail for sewing. Stuff and sew to body.

ARMS

Make 2.

Using gray yarn,

R1: Ch 2, 5 sc in second ch from hook.

R2: Sc 2 in each sc around. (10 sts)

R3–9: Sc 10, stuffing as you go.

Fasten off, leaving long tail for sewing. Stuff and sew to lights.

LEGS

Make 2.

Starting at bottom of leg and using blue or red yarn,

R1: Ch 2, 5 sc in second ch from hook.

R2: Sc 2 in each sc around. (10 sts)

R3: *Sc 1, 2 sc in next sc*, rep 5 times. (15 sts)

R4: *Sc 2, 2 sc in next sc*, rep 5 times. (20 sts)

R5: Through back loops only, *sc 2, dec 1*, rep 5 times. (15 sts)

R6: Sc 15 through back loops only.

Change to green or pink yarn.

R7: Sc 15 through back loops only

R8: Sc 15.

Change to gray yarn.

R9: Sc 15 through back loops only.

R10: *Sc 1, dec 1*, rep 5 times. (10 sts)

R11–13: Sc 10.

Fasten off, leaving a long tail for sewing. Sew to body.

LiTTLe TOYS aND THEiR HOMeS

There's something about little toys in containers that Martina just loves! She finds a little doll's hat and turns it into an even smaller doll's bed, grabs a bowl and fills it with tiny plastic animals, and carries them around in their "boat." You should have seen her face when she opened the apple home and found the little worm! She's in love with the series, and I'm sure your kids will be too!

You could also use the little fruit boxes to store little things like earrings, paper clips, and even loose change.

FiNiSHED SiZES

Pear Home: Approx 4½" tall, when closed

Snail: Approx 3" long

Apple Home: Approx 3" tall, when closed

Worm: Approx 3" long

Strawberry Home: Approx 3½" tall, when closed

Butterfly: Approx 2" tall

MaTERiaLS

Worsted-weight yarn in tan, orange, red, green, pink, yellow, black, and a tiny bit of brown

F/5 (3.75 mm) and G/6 (4 mm) crochet hooks

6 mm plastic eyes with safety backings

Black embroidery floss and tapestry needle

Fiberfill or stuffing of your choice

HOMES

Use F hook and yellow, red, or pink yarn.

BOTTOM

The bottom is the same for all the homes.

R1: Sc 2, 6 sc in second ch from hook.

R2: Sc 2 in every sc around. (12 sts)

R3: *Sc 1, 2 sc in next sc*, rep 6 times. (18 sts)

R4: *Sc 2, 2 sc in next sc*, rep 6 times. (24 sts)

R5: *Sc 3, 2 sc in next sc*, rep 6 times. (30 sts)

R6: *Sc 4, 2 sc in next sc*, rep 6 times. (36 sts)

R7: *Sc 5, 2 sc in next sc*, rep 6 times. (42 sts)

R8: *Sc 6, 2 sc in next sc*, rep 6 times. (48 sts)

R9–15: Sc 48.

R16: BPsc 48.

R17: *Sc 6, dec 1*, rep 6 times. (42 sts)

R18: Sc 42.

Fasten off and weave in end.

PEAR TOP

Using yellow yarn,

R1: Ch 2, 6 sc in second ch from hook.

R2: Sc 2 in every sc around. (12 sts)

R3: *Sc 1, 2 sc in next sc*, rep 6 times. (18 sts)

R4: Sc 18.

R5: *Sc 2, 2 sc in next sc*, rep 6 times. (24 sts)

R6 and 7: Sc 24.

R8: *Sc 3, 2 sc in next sc*, rep 6 times. (30 sts)

R9 and 10: Sc 30.

R11: *Sc 4, 2 sc in next sc*, rep 6 times. (36 sts)

R12 and 13: Sc 36.

R14: *Sc 5, 2 sc in next sc*, rep 6 times. (42 sts)

R15 and 16: Sc 42.

R17: *Sc 6, 2 sc in next sc*, rep 6 times. (48 sts)

R18–21: Sc 48.

Fasten off and weave in end.

APPLE TOP

Using red yarn,

R1: Ch 2, 6 sc in second ch from hook.

R2: Sc 2 in each sc around. (12 sts)

R3: *Sc 1, 2 sc in next sc*, rep 6 times. (18 sts)

R4: *Sc 2, 2 sc in next sc*, rep 6 times. (24 sts)

R5: *Sc 3, 2 sc in next sc*, rep 6 times. (30 sts)

R6: *Sc 4, 2 sc in next sc*, rep 6 times. (36 sts)

R7: *Sc 5, 2 sc in next sc*, rep 6 times. (42 sts)

R8: *Sc 6, 2 sc in next sc*, rep 6 times. (48 sts)

R9–15: Sc 48.

Fasten off and weave in end.

STRAWBERRY TOP

Using pink yarn,

R1: Ch 2, 6 sc in second ch from hook.

R2: Sc 2 in every sc around. (12 sts)

R3: *Sc 1, 2 sc in next sc*, rep 6 times. (18 sts)

R4: *Sc 2, 2 sc in next sc*, rep 6 times. (24 sts)

R5: *Sc 3, 2 sc in next sc*, rep 6 times. (30 sts)

R6: *Sc 4, 2 sc in next sc*, rep 6 times. (36 sts)

R7 and 8: Sc 36.

R9: *Sc 5, 2 sc in next sc*, rep 6 times. (42 sts)

R10–12: Sc 42.

R13: *Sc 6, 2 sc in next sc*, rep 6 times. (48 sts)

R14–17: Sc 48.

Fasten off and weave in ends.

PEAR AND APPLE STEM

Using brown yarn,

R1: Ch 2, 4 sc in second ch from hook.

R2–4: Sc 4.

Fasten off, leaving long tail for sewing. Sew to top of pear.

PEAR AND APPLE LEAF

Using brown yarn for pear and green yarn for apple,

R1: Ch 2, 3 sc in second ch from hook.

R2: Sc 3.

R3: Sc 2 in each sc around. (6 sts)

R4: *Sc 1, 2 sc in next sc*, rep 3 times. (9 sts)

R5 and 6: Sc 9.

R7: *Sc 1, dec 1*, rep 3 times. (6 sts)

R8: *Sk 1 sc, sc 1*, rep 3 times. (3 sts)

Fasten off, leaving long tail for sewing. Sew to stem.

STRAWBERRY LEAVES

Make 6.

Using G hook and green yarn,

R1: Ch 2, 6 sc in second ch from hook.

R2: Sc 2 in every sc around. (12 sts)

R3 and 4: Sc 12.

R5: *Sc 1, 2 sc in next sc*, rep 6 times. (18 sts)

R6 and 7: Sc 18.

Fasten off, leaving long tail for sewing. Sew open end tog and sew 6 leaves around bottom of strawberry.

SNAIL

Use G hook.

BODY

Using tan yarn,

R1: Ch 2, 6 sc in second ch from hook.

R2: Sc 2 in every sc around. (12 sts)

R3–8: Sc 12.

Work on face: Position and attach eyes, embroider mouth, and stuff face area a little.

R9–20: Sc 12.

R21: *Sk 1 sc, sc 1*, rep 6 times. (6 sts)

R22: Sc 6.

Fasten off and weave in end.

SHELL

Using orange yarn,

R1: Ch 2, 6 sc in second ch from hook.

R2: Sc 2 in every sc around. (12 sts)

R3: *Sc 1, 2 sc in next sc*, rep 6 times. (18 sts)

R4–8: Sc 18.

R9: *Sc 1, dec 1*, rep 6 times. (12 sts)

Stuff.

R10: *Sk 1 sc, sc 1*, rep 6 times. (6 sts)

Fasten off, leaving long tail to close up hole. Sew shell to tail end of body.

WORM AND BUTTERFLY

Use F hook.

WORM AND BUTTERFLY HEAD

The head is the same for both worm and butterfly.

Using green or yellow yarn,

R1: Ch 2, 6 sc in second ch from hook.

R2: Sc 2 in each sc around. (12 sts)

R3: *Sc 1, 2 sc in next sc*, rep 6 times. (18 sts)

R4: *Sc 2, 2 sc in next sc*, rep 6 times. (24 sts)

R5–11: Sc 24.

R12: *Sc 2, dec 1*, rep 6 times. (18 sts)

Work on face: Position and attach eyes; embroider mouth.

R13: *Sc 1, dec 1*, rep 6 times. (12 sts)

Stuff.

R14: *Sk 1 sc, sc 1*, rep 6 times. (6 sts)

Fasten off and weave in end.

For antennae, join green or black yarn to one side of head, ch 4, fasten off, and weave in end. Rep on other side.

WORM BODY

Make 2.

Using green yarn,

R1: Ch 2, 6 sc in second ch from hook.

R2: Sc 2 in each sc around. (12 sts)

R3–6: Sc 12.

Stuff.

R7: *Sk 1 sc, sc 1*, rep 6 times. (6 sts)

Fasten off, leaving long tail for sewing. Sew one body to head, sew second body to first body.

BUTTERFLY BODY

Using black yarn,

R1: Ch 2, 6 sc in second ch from hook.

R2: Sc 2 in each sc around. (12 sts)

R3–7: Sc 12.

Fasten off, leaving long tail for sewing. Stuff and sew to head.

BUTTERFLY WINGS

Make 2.

Using orange yarn,

R1: Ch 2, 6 sc in second ch from hook.

R2: Sc 2 in each sc around. (12 sts)

Fasten off, leaving long tail for sewing. Sew to body.

Sweet Peas

The thing with little kids and balls in my house is that the balls always end up under the couch, or they disappear! I was thinking of making some kind of container to hold the balls, and it occurred to me that it would be adorable to have sweet pea balls— and here they are, in their own container! My kids love to play with their vegetables.

Finished Sizes

Peapod: Approx 4" wide x 10" long

Peas: Approx 3" in diameter

Materials

Worsted-weight yarn in pink and two shades of green

F/5 (3.75 mm), G/6 (4 mm), and H/8 (5 mm) crochet hooks

9 mm plastic eyes with safety backings

Small piece of pink craft felt

Sewing thread and sharp needle

Black embroidery floss and tapestry needle

Fiberfill or stuffing of your choice

Peapod

Using G hook and darker shade of green yarn,

Ch 51.

R1: Sc 50 starting in second bump at back of chain (see page 77), then work 50 sc on opposite side of chain (front loops of chain). (100 sts)

R2–22: Sc 100.

Switch to F hook.

R23: Sc 100.

Fasten off and weave in end.

Peas

Make 3.

Using G hook and lighter shade of green yarn,

R1: Ch 2, 6 sc in second ch from hook.

R2: Sc 2 in each sc around. (12 sts)

R3: *Sc 1, 2 sc in next sc*, rep 6 times. (18 sts)

R4: *Sc 2, 2 sc in next sc*, rep 6 times. (24 sts)

R5: *Sc 3, 2 sc in next sc*, rep 6 times. (30 sts)

R6: *Sc 4, 2 sc in next sc*, rep 6 times. (36 sts)

R7: *Sc 5, 2 sc in next sc*, rep 6 times. (42 sts)

R8–18: Sc 42.

R19: *Sc 5, dec 1*, rep 6 times. (36 sts)

R20: *Sc 4, dec 1*, rep 6 times. (30 sts)

Work on face: Position and attach eyes; embroider mouth. For cheeks, cut 2 circles from felt and sew to head.

R21: *Sc 3, dec 1*, rep 6 times. (24 sts)

R22: *Sc 2, dec 1*, rep 6 times. (18 sts)

Stuff pea.

R23: *Sc 1, dec 1*, rep 6 times. (12 sts)

R24: Dec 6 times. (6 sts)

Fasten off, leaving long tail to close up hole, and weave in end.

Hat

Using H hook and pink yarn,

R1: Ch 2, 6 sc in second ch from hook.

R2: Sc 2 in each sc around. (12 sts)

R3: *Sc 1, 2 sc in next sc*, rep 6 times. (18 sts)

R4: *Sc 2, 2 sc in next sc*, rep 6 times. (24 sts)

R5: *Sc 3, 2 sc in next sc*, rep 6 times. (30 sts)

R6: *Sc 4, 2 sc in next sc*, rep 6 times. (36 sts)

R7: *Sc 5, 2 sc in next sc*, rep 6 times. (42 sts)

R8–15: Sc 42.

Fasten off and weave in end.

Sweet pea cheek

MUSHROOM SOFTIES

I've written this pattern for three different sizes of mushrooms, but once you make them all, it will be easy to figure out how to make even more (the pattern increases evenly).

Apart from making wonderful little friends and pincushions, they can be used as sorting toys for little kids! You could also make them in different colors (to teach colors), or sew different numbers of spots for kids to practice counting.

FINISHED SIZES

Small: Approx 2¾" tall
Medium: Approx 3" tall
Large: Approx 3½" tall

MATERIALS

Worsted-weight yarn in red and white
E/4 (3.5 mm) and F/5 (3.75) crochet hooks
6 mm plastic eyes with safety backings
Small pieces of white craft felt
Sewing thread and sharp needle
Black embroidery floss and tapestry needle
Fiberfill or stuffing of your choice

SMALL MUSHROOM

TOP

Using F hook and red yarn,

R1: Ch 2, 6 sc in second ch from hook.
R2: Sc 2 in each sc around. (12 sts)
R3: *Sc 1, 2 sc in next sc*, rep 6 times. (18 sts)
R4: *Sc 2, 2 sc in next sc*, rep 6 times. (24 sts)
R5: *Sc 3, 2 sc in next sc*, rep 6 times. (30 sts)
R6: *Sc 4, 2 sc in next sc*, rep 6 times. (36 sts)
R7–12: Sc 36.
R13: *Sc 4, dec 1*, rep 6 times. (30 sts)
R14: *Sc 3, dec 1*, rep 6 times. (24 sts)
Cut 3 circles of white felt and sew to mushroom.
R15: *Sc 2, dec 1*, rep 6 times. (18 sts)
R16: *Sc 1, dec 1*, rep 6 times. (12 sts)
Stuff.
R17: Dec 6 times, sl st 1. (6 sts)
Fasten off and weave in end.

STEM

Using E hook and white yarn,

R1: Ch 2, 5 sc in second ch from hook.
R2: Sc 2 in each sc around. (10 sts)
R3: *Sc 1, 2 sc in next sc*, rep 5 times. (15 sts)
R4: *Sc 2, 2 sc in next sc*, rep 5 times. (20 sts)
R5: *Sc 3, 2 sc in next sc*, rep 5 times. (25 sts)
R6: Through back loops only, *sc 3, dec 1*, rep 5 times. (20 sts)
R7–11: Sc 20.
Fasten off, leaving long tail for sewing.
Work on face: Position and attach eyes; embroider mouth.
Stuff and sew to top.

MEDIUM MUSHROOM

TOP

Using F hook and red yarn,

R1: Ch 2, 6 sc in second ch from hook.
R2: Sc 2 in each sc around. (12 sts)
R3: *Sc 1, 2 sc in next sc*, rep 6 times. (18 sts)
R4: *Sc 2, 2 sc in next sc*, rep 6 times. (24 sts)
R5: *Sc 3, 2 sc in next sc*, rep 6 times. (30 sts)
R6: *Sc 4, 2 sc in next sc*, rep 6 times. (36 sts)
R7: *Sc 5, 2 sc in next sc*, rep 6 times. (42 sts)
R8–14: Sc 42.
R15: *Sc 5, dec 1*, rep 6 times. (36 sts)
R16: *Sc 4, dec 1*, rep 6 times. (30 sts)
R17: *Sc 3, dec 1*, rep 6 times. (24 sts)

Cut 4 circles of white felt and sew to mushroom.

R18: *Sc 2, dec 1*, rep 6 times. (18 sts)

Stuff.

R19: *Sc 1, dec 1*, rep 6 times. (12 sts)

R20: Dec 6 times, sl st 1. (6 sts)

Fasten off and weave in end.

STEM

Using E hook and white yarn,

R1: Ch 2, 5 sc in second ch from hook.

R2: Sc 2 in each sc around. (10 sts)

R3: *Sc 1, 2 sc in next sc*, rep 5 times. (15 sts)

R4: *Sc 2, 2 sc in next sc*, rep 5 times. (20 sts)

R5: *Sc 3, 2 sc in next sc*, rep 5 times. (25 sts)

R6: *Sc 4, 2 sc in next sc*, rep 5 times. (30 sts)

R7: Through back loops only, *sc 4, dec 1*, rep 5 times. (25 sts)

R8–12: Sc 25.

Fasten off, leaving long tail for sewing.

Work on face: Position and attach eyes; embroider mouth.

Stuff and sew to top.

LARGE MUSHROOM

TOP

Using F hook and red yarn,

R1: Ch 2, 6 sc in second ch from hook.

R2: Sc 2 in each sc around. (12 sts)

R3: *Sc 1, 2 sc in next sc*, rep 6 times. (18 sts)

R4: *Sc 2, 2 sc in next sc*, rep 6 times. (24 sts)

R5: *Sc 3, 2 sc in next sc*, rep 6 times. (30 sts)

R6: *Sc 4, 2 sc in next sc*, rep 6 times. (36 sts)

R7: *Sc 5, 2 sc in next sc*, rep 6 times. (42 sts)

R8: *Sc 6, 2 sc in next sc*, rep 6 times. (48 sts)

R9–16: Sc 48.

R17: *Sc 6, dec 1*, rep 6 times. (42 sts)

R18: *Sc 5, dec 1*, rep 6 times. (36 sts)

R19: *Sc 4, dec 1*, rep 6 times. (30 sts)

R20: *Sc 3, dec 1*, rep 6 times. (24 sts)

Cut 4 circles of white felt and sew to mushroom.

R21: *Sc 2, dec 1*, rep 6 times. (18 sts)

Stuff.

R22: *Sc 1, dec 1*, rep 6 times. (12 sts)

R23: Dec 6 times, sl st 1. (6 sts)

Fasten off and weave in end.

STEM

Using E hook and white yarn,

R1: Ch 2, 5 sc in second ch from hook

R2: Sc 2 in each sc around. (10 sts)

R3: *Sc 1, 2 sc in next sc*, rep 5 times. (15 sts)

R4: *Sc 2, 2 sc in next sc*, rep 5 times. (20 sts)

R5: *Sc 3, 2 sc in next sc*, rep 5 times. (25 sts)

R6: *Sc 4, 2 sc in next sc*, rep 5 times. (30 sts)

R7: *Sc 5, 2 sc in next sc*, rep 5 times. (35 sts)

R8: Through back loops only, *sc 5, dec 1*, rep 5 times. (30 sts)

R9–13: Sc 30.

Fasten off, leaving long tail for sewing.

Work on face: Position and attach eyes; embroider mouth.

Stuff and sew to top.

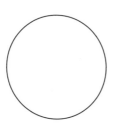

Small mushroom spot

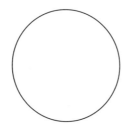

Medium mushroom spot

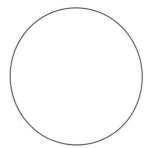

Large mushroom spot

Tea Set and Cookies

I've loved tea parties since I was a little girl, when I would go with my mom to her friend Graciela's house. She was the coolest and had a little apartment in the Ciudad Vieja neighborhood of Montevideo, full of the most amazing stuff (including a big picture of a clown that scared me). Whenever we'd go she would have a little tea party waiting for us with cookies and pastries (the best part of the tea), and they would let me have a cup of tea! I always felt like a grown-up and oh-so-important. It's funny—now, when I have tea, I feel like that little girl, sipping my tea in the cutest apartment ever and trying not to look at the clown!

Doesn't every girl love a tea party, even if it's made out of yarn?
Make one for the girl you love and have tea parties all afternoon!

FINISHED SIZES

Teapot: Approx 5" tall with lid

Sugar Bowl: Approx 3" tall with lid

Cup: Approx 3" in diameter and 2" tall

Saucer: Approx 3½" in diameter

Spoon: Approx 3" long

Cookie Plate: Approx 4¼" in diameter

Cookie: Approx 1¾" in diameter

MATERIALS

Worsted-weight yarn in blue, yellow, tan, and a tiny bit of brown

F/5 (3.75 mm) crochet hook

Tapestry needle

A tiny bit of fiberfill or stuffing of your choice (for the teapot's handle and cookies)

TEAPOT

POT

Starting with blue yarn,

R1: Ch 2, 6 sc in second ch from hook.

R2: Sc 2 in each sc around. (12 sts).

R3: *Sc 1, 2 sc in next sc*, rep 6 times. (18 sts)

R4: *Sc 2, 2 sc in next sc*, rep 6 times. (24 sts)

R5: *Sc 3, 2 sc in next sc*, rep 6 times. (30 sts)

R6: *Sc 4, 2 sc in next sc*, rep 6 times. (36 sts)

R7: *Sc 5, 2 sc in next sc*, rep 6 times. (42 sts)

R8: *Sc 6, 2 sc in next sc*, rep 6 times. (48 sts)

R9: *Sc 7, 2 sc in next sc*, rep 6 times. (54 sts)

R10: *Sc 8, 2 sc in next sc*, rep 6 times. (60 sts)

R11–17: Sc 60.

Change to yellow yarn.

R18: Sc 60.

Change to blue yarn.

R19: Sc 60.

Change to yellow yarn.

R20: Sc 60.

Change to blue yarn.

R21–23: Sc 60.

R24: *Sc 8, dec 1*, rep 6 times. (54 sts)

R25: Sc 54.

R26: *Sc 7, dec 1*, rep 6 times. (48 sts)

R27: Sc 48.

R28: *Sc 6, dec 1*, rep 6 times. (42 sts)

R29: Sc 42.

R30: BPsc 42.

R31 and 32: Sc 42.

Fasten off and weave in end.

LID

Using yellow yarn,

R1: Ch 2, 6 sc in second ch from hook.

R2: Sc 2 in each sc around (12 sts).

R3: *Sc 1, 2 sc in next sc*, rep 6 times. (18 sts)

R4: *Sc 2, 2 sc in next sc*, rep 6 times. (24 sts)

R5: *Sc 3, 2 sc in next sc*, rep 6 times. (30 sts)

R6: *Sc 4, 2 sc in next sc*, rep 6 times. (36 sts)

R7: *Sc 5, 2 sc in next sc*, rep 6 times. (42 sts)

R8–12: Sc 42.

Fasten off and weave in end.

KNOB ON LID

Using blue yarn,

R1: Ch 2, 5 sc in second ch from hook.

R2: Sc 2 in each sc around. (10 sts)

R3: *Sc 1, 2 sc in next sc*, rep 5 times. (15 sts)

R4: Sc 15.

Fasten off, leaving long tail for sewing. Sew to top of lid.

SPOUT

Using blue yarn,

R1: Leaving a long tail for sewing, ch 2, 6 sc in second ch from hook.

R2: Sc 2 in each sc around. (12 sts)

R3: *Sc 1, 2 sc in next sc*, rep 6 times. (18 sts)

R4–6: Sc 18.

R7: *Sc 1, dec 1*, rep 6 times. (12 sts)

R8–11: Sc 12.

Fasten off and weave in end. Sew closed end of spout to teapot.

HANDLE

Using blue yarn,

R1: Ch 2, 5 sc in second ch from hook.

R2: Sc 2 in each sc around. (10 sts)

R3–16: Sc 10, stuffing as you go.

Fasten off, leaving long tail for sewing. Sew to pot.

SUGAR BOWL

BOWL

Using blue yarn,

R1: Ch 2, 6 sc in second ch from hook.

R2: Sc 2 in each sc around. (12 sts)

R3: *Sc 1, 2 sc in next sc*, rep 6 times. (18 sts)

R4: *Sc 2, 2 sc in next sc*, rep 6 times. (24 sts)

R5: *Sc 3, 2 sc in next sc*, rep 6 times. (30 sts)

R6: *Sc 4, 2 sc in next sc*, rep 6 times. (36 sts)

R7: *Sc 5, 2 sc in next sc*, rep 6 times. (42 sts)

R8: *Sc 6, 2 sc in next sc*, rep 6 times. (48 sts)

R9–13: Sc 48.

Change to yellow yarn.

R14: Sc 48.

Change to blue yarn.

R15 and 16: Sc 48.

R17: BPsc 48.

R18 and 19: Sc 48.

Fasten off and weave in end.

LID

Using yellow yarn,

R1: Ch 2, 6 sc in second ch from hook.

R2: Sc 2 in each sc around (12 sts).

R3: *Sc 1, 2 sc in next sc*, rep 6 times. (18 sts)

R4: *Sc 2, 2 sc in next sc*, rep 6 times. (24 sts)

R5: *Sc 3, 2 sc in next sc*, rep 6 times. (30 sts)

R6: *Sc 4, 2 sc in next sc*, rep 6 times. (36 sts)

R7: *Sc 5, 2 sc in next sc*, rep 6 times. (42 sts)

R8: *Sc 6, 2 sc in next sc*, rep 6 times. (48 sts)

R9–13: Sc 48.

Fasten off and weave in end.

KNOB ON LID

Using blue yarn, work as for knob on teapot lid on page 69.

CUP AND SAUCER

CUP

Using blue yarn,

R1: Ch 2, 6 sc in second ch from hook.

R2: Sc 2 in each sc around. (12 sts).

R3: *Sc 1, 2 sc in next sc*, rep 6 times. (18 sts)

R4: *Sc 2, 2 sc in next sc*, rep 6 times. (24 sts)

R5: *Sc 3, 2 sc in next sc*, rep 6 times. (30 sts)

R6: *Sc 4, 2 sc in next sc*, rep 6 times. (36 sts)

R7: *Sc 5, 2 sc in next sc*, rep 6 times. (42 sts)

R8: *Sc 6, 2 sc in next sc*, rep 6 times. (48 sts)

R9–13: Sc 48.

Change to yellow yarn.

R14: Sc 48.

Change to blue yarn.

R15: Sc 48.

Change to yellow yarn.

R16: Sc 48.

Change to blue yarn.

R17–19: Sc 48.

Fasten off and weave in end.

HANDLE

Using blue yarn,

R1: Ch 2, 5 sc in second ch from hook.

R2–12: Sc 5.

Fasten off, leaving long tail for sewing. Sew to cup.

SAUCER

Using yellow yarn,

R1: Ch 2, 6 sc in second ch from hook.

R2: Sc 2 in each sc around. (12 sts).

R3: *Sc 1, 2 sc in next sc*, rep 6 times. (18 sts)

R4: *Sc 2, 2 sc in next sc*, rep 6 times. (24 sts)

R5: *Sc 3, 2 sc in next sc*, rep 6 times. (30 sts)

R6: *Sc 4, 2 sc in next sc*, rep 6 times. (36 sts)

R7: *Sc 5, 2 sc in next sc*, rep 6 times. (42 sts)

R8: *Sc 6, 2 sc in next sc*, rep 6 times. (48 sts)

R9: *Sc 7, 2 sc in next sc*, rep 6 times. (54 sts)

R10 and 11: Sc 54.

Fasten off and weave in end.

SPOON

BOWL

Using yellow yarn,

R1: Ch 2, 5 sc in second ch from hook.

R2: Sc 2 in each sc around. (10 sts)

R3: *Sc 1, 2 sc in next sc*, rep 5 times. (15 sts)

R4: Sc 15.

Fasten off and weave in end.

HANDLE

Using yellow yarn,

R1: Ch 2, 5 sc in second ch from hook.

R2–11: Sc 5.

Fasten off, leaving long tail for sewing. Sew to spoon.

COOKIE PLATE

Using yellow yarn,

R1: Ch 2, 6 sc in second ch from hook.

R2: Sc 2 in each sc around. (12 sts).

R3: *Sc 1, 2 sc in next sc*, rep 6 times. (18 sts)

R4: *Sc 2, 2 sc in next sc*, rep 6 times. (24 sts)

R5: *Sc 3, 2 sc in next sc*, rep 6 times. (30 sts)

R6: *Sc 4, 2 sc in next sc*, rep 6 times. (36 sts)

R7: *Sc 5, 2 sc in next sc*, rep 6 times. (42 sts)

R8: *Sc 6, 2 sc in next sc*, rep 6 times. (48 sts)

R9: *Sc 7, 2 sc in next sc*, rep 6 times. (54 sts)

R10: *Sc 8, 2 sc in next sc*, rep 6 times. (60 sts)

R11: *Sc 9, 2 sc in next sc*, rep 6 times. (66 sts)

Change to blue yarn.

R12: *Sc 10, 2 sc in next sc*, rep 6 times. (72 sts)

Change to yellow yarn.

R13: Sc 72.

Change to blue yarn.

R14: Sc 72.

Fasten off and weave in end.

COOKIE

Make lots!

Using tan yarn,

R1: Ch 2, 5 sc in second ch from hook.

R2: Sc 2 in each sc around. (10 sts).

R3: *Sc 1, 2 sc in next sc*, rep 5 times. (15 sts)

R4: *Sc 2, 2 sc in next sc*, rep 6 times. (20 sts)

R5: *Sc 3, 2 sc in next sc*, rep 6 times. (25 sts)

R6: Sc 25.

Fasten off, leaving long tail for sewing. Embroider chocolate chips with brown yarn.

Rep R1–6 for other side of cookie. Put 2 sides of cookie tog with WS facing, stuff slightly and sew tog.

BIRTHDAY CAKE

I made this cake right before Martina turned one so we could sing "Feliz cumpleaños," and she could practice blowing out the candle. She never learned in time (Oli didn't blow the candle on her first cake either), but they've been having a lot of fun playing pretend birthday parties with their dolls and with us!

FINISHED SIZE

Approx 8½" tall

MATERIALS

Worsted-weight yarn in yellow, white, brown, red, blue, green, tan (for the bottom), a tiny bit of orange, and a tiny bit of yellow

Size G/6 (4 mm) crochet hook

6 mm plastic eyes with safety backings

Black embroidery floss and tapestry needle

Fiberfill or stuffing of your choice

CAKE

Starting at top layer and using white yarn (frosting),

R1: Ch 2, 6 sc in second ch from hook.

R2: Sc 2 in each sc around. (12 sts).

R3: *Sc 1, 2 sc in next sc*, rep 6 times. (18 sts)

R4: *Sc 2, 2 sc in next sc*, rep 6 times. (24 sts)

R5: *Sc 3, 2 sc in next sc*, rep 6 times. (30 sts)

R6: *Sc 4, 2 sc in next sc*, rep 6 times. (36 sts)

R7: *Sc 5, 2 sc in next sc*, rep 6 times. (42 sts)

R8: *Sc 6, 2 sc in next sc*, rep 6 times. (48 sts)

R9: *Sc 7, 2 sc in next sc*, rep 6 times. (54 sts)

R10: *Sc 8, 2 sc in next sc*, rep 6 times. (60 sts)

Change to brown yarn (cake).

R11: Through back loops only, *sc 8, dec 1*, rep 6 times. (54 sts)

R12–23: Sc 54.

Change to white yarn (frosting).

R24: Through front loops only, *sc 8, 2 sc in next sc*, rep 6 times. (60 sts)

R25: *Sc 9, 2 sc in next sc*, rep 6 times. (66 sts)

R26: *Sc 10, 2 sc in next sc*, rep 6 times. (72 sts)

R27: *Sc 11, 2 sc in next sc*, rep 6 times. (78 sts)

R28: *Sc 12, 2 sc in next sc*, rep 6 times. (84 sts)

R29: *Sc 13, 2 sc in next sc*, rep 6 times. (90 sts)

R30–32: Sc 90.

Change to brown yarn (cake).

R33: Through back loops only, *sc 13, dec 1*, rep 6 times. (84 sts)

R34: *Sc 13, 2 sc in next sc*, rep 6 times. (90 sts)

R35–45: Sc 90.

Change to tan yarn (bottom of cake).

R46: Sc 90 through back loops only.

R47: *Sc 13, dec 1*, rep 6 times. (84 sts)

R48: *Sc 12, dec 1*, rep 6 times. (78 sts)

R49: *Sc 11, dec 1*, rep 6 times. (72 sts)

R50: *Sc 10, dec 1*, rep 6 times. (66 sts)

R51: *Sc 9, dec 1*, rep 6 times. (60 sts)

R52: *Sc 8, dec 1*, rep 6 times. (54 sts)

R53: *Sc 7, dec 1*, rep 6 times. (48 sts)

R54: *Sc 6, dec 1*, rep 6 times. (42 sts)

R55: *Sc 5, dec 1*, rep 6 times. (36 sts)

R56: *Sc 4, dec 1*, rep 6 times. (30 sts)

Stuff cake almost completely.

R57: *Sc 3, dec 1*, rep 6 times. (24 sts)

R58: Sc 24.

R59: *Sc 2, dec 1*, rep 6 times. (18 sts)

Finish stuffing.

R60: *Sc 1, dec 1*, rep 6 times. (12 sts)

R61: *Sk 1 sc, sc 1*, rep 6 times. (6 sts)

Fasten off and weave in end.

WHITE FROSTING EDGE

Joining white yarn to one of front loops you left in edge of top or bottom layer (right before changing to brown yarn), *4 dc in next sc, sk 1 sc, sl st 1*, rep around. Fasten off and weave in end. Repeat for second white layer.

CANDLE

Using yellow yarn,

R1: Ch 2, 6 sc in second ch from hook.

R2: Sc 2 in each sc around. (12 sts)

R3: *Sc 1, 2 sc in next sc*, rep 6 times. (18 sts)

R4: *Sc 2, 2 sc in next sc*, rep 6 times. (24 sts)

R5: *Sc 3, 2 sc in next sc*, rep 6 times. (30 sts)

R6: Through back loops only, *sc 3, dec 1*, rep 6 times. (24 sts)

R7–13: Sc 24.

Work on face: Position and attach eyes, embroider mouth.

R14: Sc 24 through back loops only.

R15: *Sc 2, dec 1*, rep 6 times. (18 sts)

R16: *Sc 1, dec 1*, rep 6 times. (12 sts)

Stuff candle.

R17: *Sk 1 sc , sc 1*, rep 6 times. (6 sts)

Fasten off and weave in end.

FLAME

Using orange yarn, ch 5, and starting at second ch from hook, sl st 1, sc 1, hdc 1, dc 1. Fasten off, leaving a tail for sewing. Embroider a tiny little bit of yellow in center of flame so it looks more "real." Sew to top of candle.

CHOCOLATE FROSTING AROUND CANDLE

Using brown yarn, ch 22, join with sl st to form a ring and then working inside ring, *hdc 1, dc 1, tr 1, tr 1, dc 1, hdc 1, sl st 1*, rep 5 more times. Fasten off, leaving long tail for sewing. Sew frosting to bottom of candle, and sew candle to cake.

STRAWBERRY

FRUIT

Make 4.

Using red yarn (pink would look nice too),

R1: Ch 2, 6 sc in second ch from hook.

R2: Sc 2 in each sc around. (12 sts)

R3 and 4: Sc 12.

R5: *Sc 1, 2 sc in next sc*, rep 6 times. (18 sts)

R6–10: Sc 18.

R11: *Sc 1, dec 1*, rep 6 times. (12 sts)

Stuff.

R12: *Sk 1 sc, sc 1*, rep 6 times. (6 sts)

Fasten off and weave in end.

LEAF

Make 4.

Using green yarn, ch 18 and join to form a ring, and then working inside of ring, *hdc 1, dc 2, hdc 1, sl st 1*, rep 6 times. Fasten off, leaving a long tail for sewing. Sew leaf to wide end of strawberry, and then sew to cake.

BLUEBERRY

Make 4.

Using blue yarn,

R1: Ch 2, 6 sc in second ch from hook.

R2: Sc 2 in each sc around. (12 sts)

R3–5: Sc 12.

Stuff.

R6: *Sk 1 sc, sc 1*, rep 6 times. (6 sts)

Fasten off, leaving long tail for sewing. Sew to cake.

GENERAL GUIDELINES

Simple crochet skills are all you need to make these delightful amigurumi.

YARN

The toys in this book are crocheted using worsted-weight yarn and a size G/6 (4 mm) crochet hook, and occasionally a size F/5 (3.75 mm), E/4 (3.5 mm) hook, or H/8 (5 mm) hook. A list of the yarn brands I used for the samples in this book can be found on page 79, but it doesn't really matter which brand you use.

Making amigurumi is a great way to use up leftover yarn. Choose colors similar to mine, or be creative and come up with your own color combinations! People often ask how many toys you can make from one 100-gram skein of worsted-weight yarn. While it varies, depending on the pattern and how tightly you crochet, I can usually get two to three of the larger animals, and many, many small toys from just one 100-gram skein of main color. Of course you'll need other colors for some body parts and embellishments.

GAUGE, TENSION, AND HOOK SIZES

The measurements given for each toy are approximate and based on the way I crochet. I crochet pretty tightly, and my gauge is as follows:

4 sts and 5 rows = 1" with G hook and worsted-weight yarn

5 sts and 6 rows = 1" with F hook and worsted-weight yarn

The finished toy size, however, isn't really that important, so don't worry if your gauge is different than mine. Depending on your tension and the yarn you use, your toys might end up being a little bit smaller or larger than the ones I made. Changing to a bigger or smaller hook will give you a bigger or smaller toy, respectively.

STITCHES

Simple stitches are used for these amigurumi projects, which make them perfect for beginners.

Chain (ch): Make a slipknot and place it on the hook. Yarn over the hook, draw the yarn through the slipknot, letting the slip knot slide off the hook. *Yarn over the hook, draw the yarn through the new loop, letting the loop slide off the hook. Repeat from * for the desired number of chains.

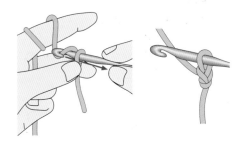

Slip Stitch (sl st): A slip stitch is used to move across one or more stitches. Insert the hook into the stitch, yarn

over the hook, and pull through both stitches at once.

Single Crochet (sc): *Insert the hook into the chain or stitch indicated, yarn over the hook, and pull through the chain or stitch (two loops remain on hook).

Yarn over the hook and pull through the remaining two loops on the hook. Repeat from * for the required number of stitches.

Back Post Single Crochet (BPsc): Insert the hook from the back around the vertical section, or post, of the single crochet stitch in the previous row, and complete the single crochet stitch as usual. Repeat as directed to a get nice, slightly raised, braid-like row of stitches.

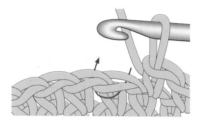

Single Crochet Increase: Work two single crochet stitches into the same stitch.

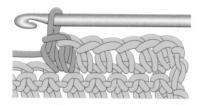

Single Crochet Decrease (dec): (Insert the hook into the next stitch, yarn over, pull up a loop) twice; yarn over and pull through all three loops on the hook.

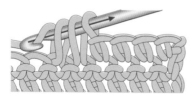

Half Double Crochet (hdc): *Yarn over the hook, insert the hook into the chain or stitch indicated. Yarn over the hook and pull through the stitch (three loops remain on the hook).

Yarn over the hook and pull through all three loops on the hook. Repeat from * for the required number of stitches.

Double Crochet (dc): *Yarn over the hook, insert the hook into the chain or stitch indicated. Yarn over the hook and pull through the stitch (three loops are on the hook); yarn over the hook and pull through two loops on the hook (two loops remain on the hook).

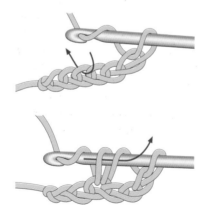

Yarn over the hook and pull through the remaining two loops on the hook (one loop remains on the hook). Repeat from * for the required number of stitches.

Triple Crochet (tr): *Yarn over the hook twice, insert the hook into the chain or stitch indicated. *Yarn over the hook and pull through the stitch (four loops on the hook); yarn over the hook and pull through two loops on the hook (three loops remain on the hook).

Yarn over the hook and pull through two loops on the hook) twice (one loop remains on the hook). Repeat from * for the required number of stitches.

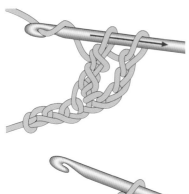

WORKING IN CHAIN LOOPS

When crocheting the first row into the beginning chain, the first row of stitches is generally worked into one or both loops on the right side of the chain.

Crocheting into top loop

Crocheting into both loops

For some projects, the first row of stitches is worked in the "bump" on the wrong side of the chain.

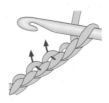

WORKING IN STITCH LOOPS

The majority of the stitches are worked in both loops of the stitches from the previous row. There are a few projects where you will work a row into the back loop or the front loop of the stitch.

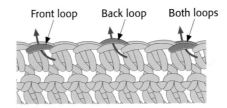

Front loop   Back loop   Both loops

CROCHETING IN THE ROUND

When crocheting in the round, I crochet around and around, forming a continuous spiral. To keep track of where the rounds begin and end you can mark the end or beginning of a round with a safety pin, stitch marker, or little piece of yarn pulled through one of the stitches. At the end of the last round, slip stitch in the first single

crochet of the previous round and fasten yarn off.

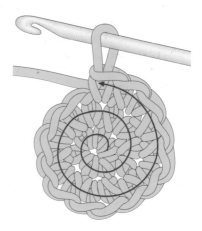

HOW TO CHANGE YARN COLORS

Some projects require alternating two colors in the body. To do this, work the last stitch of a round until one step remains in the stitch; then work the last step with the new color and continue the round in the new color. Continue to the end of the round and change color in the same matter.

ADDING FACES

Although I have used plastic eyes with safety backings on all of the toys, you can instead embroider the eyes, use buttons, or cut out and sew on little pieces of felt. For each pattern, eye sizes are given in millimeters.

The templates for the muzzles and any other pieces to be cut from felt are included with each project. Cut the felt pieces with sharp scissors to get nice, smooth edges. Using embroidery floss and a needle, I use simple stitches to "draw" the faces on the felt before attaching the felt pieces to the face. Sew pieces of felt on with a sharp needle and matching sewing thread using a very small running stitch close to the edge of the piece.

Mouths: For a simple mouth, bring the needle out at point A, insert the needle at point B, leaving a loose strand of yarn to form the mouth. Once you're happy with the shape of the mouth, bring the needle out again at point C, cross over the loose strand of yarn, and insert the needle at point D to make a tiny stitch. Secure ends on wrong side.

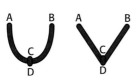

Satin stitch noses and eyes: Bring needle out through point A, insert at point B, and repeat, following the shape you want for the nose or eyes and making sure to work stitches really close together. Secure the ends on the wrong side.

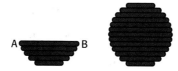

Another option for embroidering a nose is to work from a center point upward. Bring the needle up from underneath at point A; insert the needle at point B. Bring the needle up at point C, very close to point A. Insert the needle back into point B. Continue working stitches close to each other to create a triangle, making sure to always insert the needle back into point B. When you are satisfied with the triangle, make two long stitches across the top of the nose to help define it.

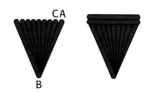

BACKSTITCH

Embroider lines on the turtle shell on page 37 using a backstitch.

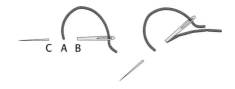

STUFFING

Stuff your toys firmly so they retain their shape and don't look "droopy." Be careful not to overstuff them, though, because the stuffing will stretch the fabric and may show through the stitches.

I always use polyester fiberfill stuffing because it's nonallergenic, won't bunch up, and it's washable, which is always good when you're making toys! If you do wash the toys, make sure you follow the yarn care instructions on the label.

JOINING THE EXTREMITIES

I always use a tapestry needle and the same color yarn as the pieces (or at least one of the pieces) that I want to join together. When sewing pieces to the body, make sure they are securely attached so that little fingers can't pull them off.

On some animals the opening of the extremities will remain open for sewing onto the body; the instructions will tell you when to leave them open. Position the piece on the body and sew all around it, going through the front stitches of both the extremity and the body.

On other animals, the opening of the extremities will be sewn closed before being attached to the body. To do this, pinch the opening closed, line up the stitches of one side with the other side, and sew through the front loop of one side and the back loop of the other side. Position the piece where you want it on the body and sew.

ABBREVIATIONS AND GLOSSARY

*	repeat directions between * and * as many times as indicated	**hdc**	half double crochet	**sk**	skip
BPsc	back post single crochet	**R**	round(s)	**sl st**	slip st
ch	chain	**rem**	remaining	**st(s)**	stitch(es)
dc	double crochet	**rep**	repeat	**tog**	together
dec	decrease (see "Single Crochet Decrease" on page 76)	**rnd**	round	**tr**	triple crochet
		sc	single crochet		

RESOURCES

CARON

www.caron.com

LION BRAND YARN

www.lionbrand.com

PATONS

www.patonsyarns.com

RED HEART

www.coatsandclark.com

SAFETY EYES

Your local craft store probably carries safety eyes. If you can't find them locally, visit www.sunshinecrafts.com; search for "eyes." They ship them fast.

If you want fun, colorful eyes, check out www.suncatchereyes.net.

About the Author

Ana Paula Rímoli was born in Montevideo, Uruguay, where she was always making stuff. She started crocheting when she was little, sitting outside one summer afternoon with her neighbor lending instruction. She started with scarves and granny squares and little bags and never stopped. When her oldest daughter was born, she started crocheting little toys for her and later discovered amigurumi. Ana's been "hooked" ever since, and the toy collection is growing and growing, slowly taking over the whole house!

Ana now lives in New Jersey with her two little girls and never-ending sources of inspiration, Oli and Martina, and her super-nice husband who supports her yarn obsession.